A Brief Wondrous Life

A Brief Wondrous Life

A Novel

Mary Ann Peterson

First Edition: September 2010 printed by NorthStar Press
Reprinted: February 2017

Printed in the United States of America

Reprinted by
FuzionPrint
1250 E 115th Street
Burnsville, MN 55337

"My candle burns at both ends;
It will not last the night;
But ah, my foes, and oh, my friends
It gives a lovely light"
-Edna St. Vincent Millay

Concerning the rewards and pitfalls of her profession, renowned poet, Edna St. Vincent Millay, once remarked, "A person who publishes a book willfully appears before the populace with his pants down...If it is a good book nothing can hurt him. If it is a bad book, nothing can help him."

Chapter One

This wasn't Jennie Roger's first train trip to Quincy, but it would be the most memorable trip she has taken to her hometown. The trip to attend her class of 1960 high school reunion changed her life forever.

Creeping through the underground tunnels of Union Station, the train changed tracks and made its way through city intersections, passing haunted-looking, old factory buildings as it left Chicago and Western Avenues on the way to Cicero, the first stop going west. The next stop would be Berwyn, then LaGrange, Naperville and Aurora, the last stop in the metropolitan area. Jennie Rogers had made this trip often, and she recognized all nine stops on the Burlington route to Quincy. The train rocked and swayed as they crept through the western suburbs, and the cup of coffee she had brought on board sloshed from side to side. She picked it up and took a sip, not realizing it had now become lukewarm. She was going home to Quincy to attend her class of 1960's ten-year reunion, and that was foremost on her mind.

Her fiancé, Steve Hollis, had brought her to Union Station to see her off. He had proposed marriage, but even though they have been constant companions for over a year, Jennie wasn't sure about marriage. Steve wanted to accompany her, but she wanted to attend this class reunion by herself even though she knew she would probably be the only single person there. She wondered if this separation would make the decision easier. Her mother couldn't understand why she had reservations about getting married.

After leaving Aurora the train again picked up speed, and as she glanced out the window, the all-too-familiar Illinois countryside quickly absorbed her attention. The same red barns, stately silos, and munching black-and white-cows dotted the landscape. Roadside stands with mounds of pumpkins and bushels of red apples added color to the surrounding tawny fields. It was October, and the crops had been harvested leaving barren fields waiting for a cover of snow.

She didn't want the rest of her coffee, and wanting an excuse to get up and move around, she steadfastly walked down the aisle looking for a place to deposit the half-filled Styrofoam cup. This was homecoming weekend at most schools, and the car was crowded with laughing, boisterous college students. With her youthful good looks and casual attire of T-shirt and jeans, she could easily have been taken for a student herself. She smiled and acknowledged a boy's whistle of admiration.

As the train slowed and eased into the station in Quincy, she scanned the crowd of people gathered on the platform looking for the familiar face of her best friend in school. Not seeing her, Jennie reflected on her friend's tradition of tardiness: a lovable scatterbrain, she was always late and on the run.

"Jennie, Jennie, here I am," she heard someone in the crowd cry out, and sure enough there was Lynn running breathlessly through the station to meet her. Lynn was an attractive dishwater blonde with hazel eyes, and the ponytail of her youth was now pulled back in a fashionable French twist. Jennie called it "her sophisticated look." Lynn had always been a little on the chunky side (big-boned, her mother said), but her 5'7" height and her "beanpole" husband's height diminished it. They hugged and looked at each other as if it was their first meeting.

"How do you stay slim and trim?" asked Lynn.

Jennie replied, "How do you always look like the happiest person alive?"

"It's because I'm married to a wonderful man."

Inwardly, Jennie wondered if she was going to cajole her into getting married.

Still panting from running, Lynn said, "I have been at the Holiday Inn all morning decorating. I was so afraid of being late and missing you."

"There's a Wendy's just a couple of blocks from here. Let's stop for coffee and a bite to eat before I take you home."

"Yes, let's," Jennie said. She had a million things to discuss such as what to wear to the dinner-dance tomorrow night.

"I was elected chairman of the reunion planning committee, and we have been very busy with decorations and reminiscences of our high school years."

"Well, you are the most qualified person for the job. What's the plan?" Jennie replied.

"We've have taken several pictures from the yearbook and had them blown up, and they are placed on the walls around the dining room. We tried to have all the students included. Everyone likes to look at pictures and reminisce about old times. Of course, blue and white is the color scheme, and the school spirit is everywhere," Lynn continued.

"What about the dinner?" Jennie asked.

"The Holiday Inn will serve a roast beef dinner, and there'll be an open bar before dinner. We've arranged to have the jazz band from Quincy University play for the dance; they'll play pop music and jazz. They're really good," Lynn said.

"You've been busy, it sounds like a wonderful evening," Jennie replied.

"Incidentally, I didn't expect to see a Wendy's in Quincy. When did that happen?"

"About a year ago. The farmers are selling their family farms, and the town is really growing. First Wal-Mart came and then Kmart. The sad thing is they all offer the same lower prices for lower quality products – and it's probably all made in China. The fast food chains followed the discount stores."

"Yes, I know," Jennie said, "It's happening everywhere."

As Lynn was driving Jennie to her mother's home, they drove down Main Street through town. Jennie smiled at seeing the old Blue Moon Café with its swinging blue moon for a sign, the Ben Franklin, Walters Dry Goods, and Lucille's Hat Shop. How little things have changed in ten years, she thought. As they neared the high school, a cluster of teenage girls crossed the street without looking and without a care in the world. Lynn had to brake suddenly as the girls in snug jeans, oversized sweaters, and bright red lipstick, walked in front of her car as if it wasn't there.

"Did we act that way when we were their age?" Jennie asked.

"I can't recall, but we probably did. Do you remember when some of the boys in class climbed the water tower one night and painted "Class of 1960" in bright orange? Well, it's still there."

"Yes, I remember that; everyone was amazed that it could be done. The class of 1960 made history. I'm surprised it hasn't been painted over by now," Jennie replied.

"Maybe that's why it hasn't been removed; the sheer complexity that it took to get up there is something to be hailed."

Jennie's mother was overjoyed to see her and her first remark was, "You're too thin," followed by "How is Steve? I wish he would have come with you."

"Mother, Steve wanted to come with me, he wanted to see you too, but I want to attend this class reunion by myself."

"Well, I just don't think you will find anyone nicer than Steve." Jennie smiled and changed the subject.

Saturday morning dawned quietly, no lawnmowers humming on homecoming weekend. She hurriedly got out of bed and began brushing her teeth, eager to start the day. It was perfect football weather – cool, but sunny. A full day of activities was planned starting with a tailgate lunch of brats and burgers, then the game with Macomb, Quincy's biggest rival. Lynn said Quincy was favored to win, but they were closely matched, so anything can happen. Jennie planned to attend the game with Lynn and her husband, Roger, who has a State Farm insurance agency. They went steady all through high school and married after college. Now, she runs his insurance office. That seemed a little smothering to Jennie, but they were a perfect pair.

They took their seats in the stadium just as the Blue Devil's mascot led the team onto the field. The stadium was awash with blue and white and roaring students. Jennie closely watched the cheerleaders go through their routines and felt a wave of nostalgia and envy as she recalled her days as the lead cheerleader at Quincy High. She still had her blue sweater with white letters. The band played the same music, but today it sounded peppier and louder. As Quincy took the lead at 21-14 in the fourth quarter, the students went wild, and the cheerleaders were too hoarse to cheer, so they did calisthenics. There would not be any long faces at the dinner-dance tonight.

After a rousing football game, everyone was in an exuberant mood as they headed for the Holiday Inn for dinner and an evening of dancing. Lynn wore a long skirt and blouse and looked smashing. Jennie wore a Mary Quant black mini dress with platform shoes and was gorgeous. Her classmates showed up at the cocktail hour before dinner with shrieks and laughter as they recognized one another, saying, "Oh my God! You look great" or "You haven't changed a bit." Then they dove in for a closer look at the little yearbook picture pinned to their dress as if to affirm their remark. Jennie learned she wasn't the only single person; her marital status was shared by another girl and a boy in the class who were both absent. Probably chickened out because they knew everyone else would be married, she thought.

Everyone recalled their years at Quincy High with a mixture of embarrassment and humor as they swapped notes on college, clothing fads and haircuts (or lack of), drugs and dating. They had all been eighteen once, and their attitude was, "Hey, we were all in this together." They gleefully recounted the Friday and Saturday nights when the boys cruised up and down the eight blocks of Main Street honking and whistling at the girls they passed along the way. This went on for hours. Usually, they all ended up at the Dairy Queen which was the summer hangout.

At dinner, Jennie was seated at a table with her former boyfriend, David, and his wife. She was surprised to see that he was practically bald and wondered how a person can go bald in ten years. Steve has beautiful hair and a lot of it. When David asked her to dance, she wished he was someone else. As the evening wore on, her joyful mood turned to sadness, and the people around her became faceless as her thoughts drifted back to Steve. She missed Steve's presence and the safe and secure feeling of having him at her side. In the crowded room she felt terribly alone, and she wished that Steve had come with her. She was anxious to see him, and she hoped he would surprise her and meet her train in Chicago tomorrow afternoon, even though they hadn't discussed it.

Chapter Two

Sunday morning Jennie eagerly boarded the Burlington for the four-hour train ride back to Chicago. Her fellow passengers were not the jubilant students on her previous trip, and she missed their gaiety.

She leaned back and gazed out the window at the fleeting countryside as she reflected on the evening's events and how she wished Steve had been with her. To free her mind from the guilty feeling she had for not wanting him to accompany her, she picked up the Quincy newspaper she brought along to pass time. Before long the train was nearing Aurora and the Chicago metropolitan area. She felt the train brake as it slowly made its way through the western suburbs until finally creeping through the underground tunnels and screeching to a halt in Union Station.

As the train jerked to a final stop, Jennie scanned the platform hoping to see Steve waiting for her. Disappointed, she grabbed her bag and made her way up the escalator to the street level and waved at the first taxicab in line to take her to her apartment in Lincoln Park. When she entered, she immediately sensed a feeling of emptiness in her life.

It isn't supposed to be this way, she thought, and for the first time she had an uneasy feeling about her relationship with Steve. She unpacked her bag, showered and snuggled into the big cushy chair that always gave her a feeling of security.

While waiting for the phone to ring, her thoughts went back to their first meeting. It took place at a funeral for a young man who was a close friend of Steve and a colleague of hers at work. She was seated next to Steve, and after the service they chatted and disclosed their relation to the deceased. The deceased and Steve had been good friends in college, as were several other preppy looking guys seated in the same row. They decided to continue the conversation at lunch, and their friendship had endured for over a year.

Her eyes turned to her favorite photo, framed and placed on the table next to her chair. It was taken the day Steve graduated from the University of Minnesota. His navy blue blazer coordinated perfectly with his blue button-down shirt, and silk regimental stripe tie. His was not the dress of a typical accountant; he dressed with style, and he exuded confidence. His lips were parted suggesting a smile or the hint of a mischievous remark about to be uttered. Steve was a good-looking, fun-loving man.

The ringing of her doorbell startled her back to reality. Denise, her neighbor down the hall, smiled and walked past Jennie inviting herself in.

"I can't believe you're alone. Where's Steve?"

Jennie faltered, and wistfully said, "I don't know, I'm waiting for him to call."

"I'm hungry. Aren't you? Let's go have a pizza."

"Okay, Jennie replied, I'm getting hungry, too. Let's walk down to Tony's but let's not stay long in case Steve stops by."

Tony's was an unpretentious neighborhood pub and grill. The atmosphere was casual and friendly, making everyone feel at home. For many customers, it was a second home. Jennie and her friends liked it because it was a place where they could go without a date. They served a full menu, but the younger crowd went there for its pizza. It had lots of dark wood with interesting beer signs and artifacts on the walls. On weekends, when they had live bands, it was really crowded, but no one really minded.

It seemed everyone in Lincoln Park decided to go to Tony's as the place was jammed. Normally, there was a line, but it moved fast so you never really had to wait. However, tonight, Jennie and Denise were told there would be a thirty minute wait, so they went into the bar where there was standing room only. They each ordered a glass of beer. They looked around for familiar faces, and Denise pointed to a booth in the corner where a man and woman were seated, saying "Isn't that Steve?"

Jennie abruptly turned to look at the same time Steve's glance was in her direction. She stood transfixed and had a look of horror when their eyes met. Instinctively, she turned and ran from the room.

The next day Steve called her at work and said, "It wasn't what it looked like."

Before he could continue, Jennie snapped, "Well, what do you call it?" and hung up.

Steve called back and said, "We need to talk, I'll be there at seven.

Her doorbell rang promptly at seven, and when she opened the door Steve tried to take her into his arms, but she brushed him aside. He walked past her and sat in his usual chair.

In a hurt, faltering voice, he asked, "How was the reunion, how is your mother, was your old boyfriend there?

"Steve, mother is fine, she asked about you, and, yes, David was there, but he is married now, and we have no feelings toward each other. I danced with him, but he meant nothing to me."

"When you told me you weren't ready for marriage and you didn't want me to go with you to your high school reunion, I assumed there was someone else in your life. Is there someone else, Jennie?" Jennie felt terribly guilty. She couldn't think of a reasonable reason why she didn't want him to go with her. At the time it seemed logical, but now it seemed so unimportant, and she tried to explain her feelings, assuring him there wasn't anyone else, that she missed him at the reunion and wished that he was there. Even though she has apprehensions about marriage, it's not because she didn't love him.

"Steve, there isn't anyone I would rather be with than you, but I'm just not ready for marriage yet. I wish we could always live as we have this past year – together and extremely happy."

"Jennie, I love you, and I want to be with you forever. I'll wait for you as long as it takes for you to say "yes."

Steve was Catholic, and extremely good-looking with short curly brown hair and dark brown piercing eyes. He was very intelligent with a reckless, vibrant attitude; his quiet smile at times is slightly wicked, irresistible. Heads turned wherever he went, and naturally Jennie was attracted to him.

They often had interesting discussions about religion and life in general. He did not attend church regularly, but observed all holidays.

Jennie was Presbyterian and was also not a regular churchgoer, but, like Steve, she observed holidays. They did not feel their religious differences would prevent them from marrying and decided that neither would change their religion. However, Jennie, on occasion, accompanied Steve when he went to Mass, but he has never attended services at her church. He was complacent with his beliefs, so religion wasn't an issue as far as he was concerned. For the time being, this was not a problem for Jennie, but at times she thought about raising their children in church. Shouldn't they be thinking beyond themselves? Was this the reason "she isn't ready for marriage yet?"

Steve then broke the news and told her he received a good job offer from the State of Arizona in Phoenix which he was seriously thinking of accepting, and he wanted her to join him after he got settled. Jennie consented, but she hoped his decision wasn't an impulsive one because of their falling-out over the reunion, although it wasn't a surprise that he mentioned the job offer in Phoenix. His father is in the construction business and was planning a housing development in the Phoenix area, so his parents moved there a year ago. Steve was plagued with allergies from which he suffered severe asthma attacks. He said half his childhood was spent in bed being consoled by the hiss of a vaporizer, and it was his asthma that exempted him from the Vietnam War. His parents had been encouraging Steve and Jennie to come to Arizona for health reasons. Steve, an accountant, just recently received his CPA license. He had been pursuing job offers since he passed the test.

They spent the next two weeks together trying not to think of their separation, but assuring each other they would be in constant communication. Tears rolled down Jennie's cheeks as his plane taxied down the runway.

Steve wrote that he was becoming acclimated to his job. He told her that finally he could breathe easily; his asthma might be an illness of the past. She would like the climate, it was dry, and now in March it was 70 degrees. He had difficulty getting used to it – he wanted to be outside instead of being tied to his desk. Steve played tennis at every opportunity, but those were becoming fewer and fewer. He tried various Mexican dishes and liked the food. There was year-round sunshine. Nearly every place was air conditioned. He knew she will like it here.

Steve headed up the Accounting Department, and it wasn't long before he discovered there were discrepancies in records concerning the bidding of construction jobs, which he referred to as "dangling carrots." As a result, one large state project had a huge cost overrun of more than $10 million and was far behind schedule. He immediately recommended an audit and a thorough examination of the accounting records. It consumed so much of his time that his workday extended well into the evening. This startling discovery did not leave much time for personal matters, and initially his infrequent letters did not alarm Jennie.

Jennie's job with Bradley Engineering Company in Chicago was also taking new dimensions. A fellow engineer left the firm, and in lieu of replacing him, many of his responsibilities were given to Jennie. With her increased workload, she was very busy and some days had only time enough to send a brief note to Steve. This continued, and she was hearing from him less and less frequently. Her first thought was that he had met someone else, but she quickly shrugged off that morbid thought. In his most recent letter he mentioned because of recent complications, he would not be able to communicate with her until certain circumstances changed. He sounded very secretive. He also told her not to expect to come to Phoenix soon and maybe not at all. She became alarmed and tried contacting him, but her letters went unanswered. She thought everything he said was so vague. Was she supposed to read between the lines?

Jennie had no way of knowing the mafia had infiltrated the State's construction projects, and it was necessary that Steve function with the utmost secrecy.   Even his parents and most trusted employees were not aware of the investigations. He was given a new identity while assisting and cooperating with the FBI, and he was not allowed to discuss anything with anyone. He was constantly in danger since he was warned that anyone who challenged the mafia might be assassinated or gunned down without warning.   Steve was unknowingly up against a formidable opposition. Finally, she received a short note that cleared her mind somewhat. It started out, "I love you very much and want to be with you as soon as possible, but I don't know when that will be. Always know that I love you!"

While at work she didn't have time to dwell upon this sudden mysterious turn of events, but in the evening when she was alone, she found herself rehashing the suspicions contained in the brief notes she has received from him.   She wished she knew what was going on and why Steve made the remark, 'Always know that I love you.' It sounded so final, like he was saying good-bye. If only she could contact him, but he had told her she shouldn't, and to try would only cause problems for him. She had to trust him, that everything would be okay, and soon she would discover that her worries were baseless speculation.

A week later when she nonchalantly switched on the television to catch the CBS evening news, Walter Cronkite was talking about organized crime in the construction business in Phoenix. She stood there, absolutely riveted, taking in his every word. He told of a person named Steve Hollis who was going to be an expert witness in a trial against organized crime in state construction projects, but was gunned down the day before he was to testify. She broke down and sobbed hysterically while trying to listen to the broadcast.

In cooperation with the FBI, Steve had discovered that organized crime groups had infiltrated several state construction projects. They were extorting money from construction contractors and they were involved in bid-rigging through construction and cement-pouring bids.

He was asked to be an expert witness because of his thorough knowledge of the State's accounting records, and he was given protection under the Federal Witness Protection Program, but the day before he was to testify before a county grand jury, he was gunned down gangland style on a stairwell in a parking garage. Cronkite said he was shot with a .22 caliber gun, and there were five bullet holes in his body and a dime was placed on his forehead.

Jennie was astounded at what she was hearing and seeing on the nationwide television newscast, and she thought about Steve's secrecy and what little she knew about his job. She was too shocked and dazed to comprehend everything she was hearing, and she tried to make sense of it; he wasn't a threat to anyone; he was only trying to do his job and live a simple life. He didn't deserve to die! Then the television picture changed from Cronkite to the stairwell, and they showed a close-up of his crumpled body lying in a pool of blood at the foot of the stairs. At the sight of his body lying in a pool of blood, she began screaming at the top of her lungs, shouting no, no, no, and she sobbed uncontrollably for what seemed like hours until she could cry no more.

Chapter Three

When the plane was airborne, the woman sitting next to her politely asked if she was also going to Phoenix to escape Chicago's Siberia-like weather. Jennie smiled and matter-of-factly stated, "No, I'm going to attend my fiance's memorial service." The woman quietly murmured, "I'm so sorry" and picked up her book. Barely audible, Jennie said "thank you," and, with a gesture of finality, turned to the window. She was not in the mood to share her sorrow with a stranger.

Again, her thoughts went back to their first meeting – strangers attending the funeral of a mutual friend. Now, she was on her way to Phoenix to attend Steve's memorial service. She wondered if she would be able to get through it and have the strength to smile and greet people. All she wanted to do is mourn in her own way, alone and silently.

She recalled her own mother's sadness and her remark about wishing Steve would have come with her to her high school reunion so they would have had more time together. Jennie wondered if he had gone with her if he would be alive today. Will I ever get over these feelings of guilt and regret for not wanting him to go to the reunion with me!

She turned to look at a man coming down the aisle and was surprised to see Larry Carlson, a friend of Steve's. He and Steve grew up together and played tennis together. He beckoned her to join him so she turned to the woman next to her and excused herself so she could stand. They discussed plans to go to Steve's parent's home. He had a rental car waiting and they could go together. Jennie agreed to meet him at the departure gate. She returned to her seat, and before long, the flight attendant came on the intercom: "We are lowering our altitude and will be circling Phoenix shortly. Fasten your seat belts and put your trays in the upright position." Soon the huge 747's wheels lightly touched the tarmac and rolled to a stop at the gate. Everyone rose to retrieve their carry-ons from the overhead bins. Jennie waited at the departure gate for Larry.

Larry bounded down the ramp, picked up her bag and pointed to the rental car sign. It was a sunny, hot 82 degrees in Phoenix, and they shed their coats and reveled in the delightful change of temperature. On their way to the Hollis home, they discussed Steve's job and how exhausting and perilous it became after discovering the involvement of organized crime in their construction projects. Jennie told Larry about the secrecy surrounding his job, "He didn't tell me he had decided to become a federal witness and testify at an upcoming trial. He thought I would worry unnecessarily. He did everything the federal investigators asked him to do not fully realizing how dangerous the situation could become. I wish I could have been there with him."

Jennie embraced Mr. and Mrs. Hollis, and together they silently wept. She couldn't hold back the tears that gushed forth as she looked at a picture of Steve and her which was placed on a table. Jim Hollis kissed her on her forehead, and Grace Hollis guided her around the room introducing her to family and friends.

His parents decided to postpone the memorial service to accommodate their many friends and family from out of town. They were invited to the Hollis home after the service for refreshments. Jennie helped the other ladies prepare casseroles and salads to appease the hungry mourners. Guests brought food, made drinks and set plates on the dining room table for as many who were present at the time. Soon sadness seemed to give way to lightness. Steve's parents were beginning to heal and cope with the loss of their son, and they gained strength from the many guests who surrounded them.

Jennie stayed on longer to console Steve's parents. They would need all the strength they could muster in the months ahead to get through the investigations and aftermath of Steve's death. It was already evident that every aspect of Steve's life would read like an open book. She now understood his secrecy and his lack of communication – he didn't want to leave a paper trail to her or his parents in the event that he would be exposed as an informant. He had to be especially vigilant and protective of his parents. Now they would have to share the limelight with Steve. One evening as they were watching the evening news, the announcer speculated about how an unknown person could have been hunted down like prey in the wild, and why four hundred mourners attended the memorial service for an obscure newcomer.

It raised questions: Was it finally public outcry over the increasing evidence of mafia activity in Arizona? Would their outrage become the force needed to put an end to the senseless murders and put the criminals behind bars for once and for all? Didn't Steve have the protection of a U.S. Marshall as all participants in the Witness Security Program are entitled? Did Steve have to become a martyr? The answers to these questions and many others would be demanded by the media in ongoing investigations.

The media were relentless; it seemed a reporter stepped out of nowhere whenever Grace and Jim left their home, and a photographer was not far behind. Because Steve was their son, they wondered if the mafia was also scrutinizing their every move, and they contemplated leaving Phoenix for awhile. Their daily life was becoming too painful and too stressful – it was like adding salt to an open wound. Mark, their younger son, was in school at the University of Denver; perhaps they would go there for a visit. Relatives elsewhere encouraged them to visit.

Larry had taken an earlier flight back to Chicago, and Jennie was glad to be traveling alone to collect her own thoughts and reflect on the past year with Steve. She took from her purse the obituary with accompanying photo that had been clipped from the Phoenix newspaper and studied it as if he was gazing at her alone. She recalled their first meeting, and she remembers the shiver of excitement and joy she felt the first time he called her. She remembered his shyness when they began dating and how he avoided being close and romantic even though she was sure he was as attracted to her as she was to him. One night she invited him over for dinner, and he was barely inside the door when she impulsively threw her arms around him and kissed him. He responded with a kiss that had them undressing as they made their way to the bedroom.

From then on, they were always together. She didn't go any place without him. They teased each other and sometimes bickered and quarreled, but they always made up. It was the making up that kept them together.

He became very possessive of her, not in a dominating, controlling way, it was more like "you are my girl, and we belong together." She loved it and felt the same way toward him. She liked knowing he would always be there to protect her. He was very protective of his brother, Mark, too.

She will always remember summers with Steve; they took advantage of everything summer had to offer. They took long walks around the lake and then sat on the beach talking while taking in the beauty of Lake Michigan. Sometimes he became very quiet and introspective while gazing at the tranquil, endless-expanse of water, and mere conversation couldn't bring him out of his reverie. It was as if he was in his own little world, and she wasn't allowed to enter.

The day before Steve was scheduled to take the test for his CPA license they spent the afternoon at the beach studying for the test. While lying in the sand on the deserted beach, she kissed him and hoped the day's cramming would pay off. Steve drew her close and said, "It will, you will bring me luck.

After spending hot Saturday afternoons at the beach, they went home and took long cool showers. She would slip into a floor-length skirt and sandals, while Steve donned a cool, patterned sport shirt. After dinner they danced and laughed forgetting about their sun-burned backs and shoulders.

Steve's parents entertained fairly often, and they tried not to miss their lavish parties where champagne flowed freely, and she had her first taste of caviar.

On warm summer evenings after arriving home from work they couldn't wait to get into their shorts and walking shoes and jog on the bicycle path around Lake Michigan. Sometimes they took off their shoes and waded in the water along the shore while the undercurrent lapped at their ankles. They were young, and their life was a happy, carefree existence.

On their last night together, they watched the sunset and had a cocktail. For a few hours they were their usual happy selves looking out toward the water not thinking of anything but being together, trying not to think of tomorrow.

Then she recalled saying good-bye at the airport. They hugged and kissed then stood together for a long time until they heard the final boarding call. It was the last time he held her in his arms, and sometimes she can still feel the warmth of his body next to hers.

When she arrived home and entered the front door, a startling reflection appeared in the hall mirror. Her face looked tired, and her long brown hair looked limp and lifeless. Her once-sparkling eyes looked despondent and swollen from weeping.

She studied her image and thought about her future. Steve is gone. She will have to put her life back together again by herself. She knows Steve would tell her to stop mourning, and get on with life. A dream world has ended, and now she has to live in the real one.

She decided to go to the beauty shop for a trim and some highlights. She will get some new eye makeup. She flipped through a fashion magazine extolling products for naturally smooth skin and perfect manicures, then tossed it aside and jumped in the shower. Her monthly magazines couldn't help her with this decision.

After a long relaxing shower, Jennie wrapped a thick white towel around her and carefully began doing her toe nails. Her legs were shaved perfectly smooth. She had little puffs of cotton separating each toe as she applied the undercoat, then the scarlet nail polish and a top coat. The pedicure was almost therapeutic as she contemplated her future and her life-long desire to be a writer.

Wanting to look like a student, she pulled on a sexy black, long-sleeved T-shirt and boot-cut jeans. She plugged in the hair dryer and blew enough hot air into her glossy brown hair to give it some volume. Her 5'6" slender figure looked chic and fashionable. Now she would turn heads again. Her life would be taking a new direction; she was going back to school.

She enrolled in an evening creative writing class at Columbia College. Columbia is one of the largest arts colleges in the U.S., specializing in fiction writing and poetry. Jennie wanted to step into her life the way it was ten years ago when she was still in school. She knew Columbia was well-known for its creative writing program, and she wanted more than anything to become a good writer. She dreamed of being a best-selling author; she wanted talent, fame and money.

Jennie quickly made friends with Suzanne Stein, a fellow student, who was a fan of Cervantes and Bob Dylan. After class, they began going to a coffee house called, "The Quorum," ordering mugs of Costa Rican coffee or cherry cokes and discussing politics, writing, music, and men. The Quorum had a homey atmosphere where students came to study and read, or just hang out. Everybody was on a first name basis. Local artist's paintings decorated the walls and comfy leather sofas, plush carpeting and a fireplace made it the student's favorite place to hang out, and it was always crowded. On Monday nights a psychic came and gave readings for $5 for a 5-minute read. Wednesday nights was poetry night, and Suzanne and other student poets read their poetry aloud to a rapt audience. Suzanne always asked Brian, the owner of the coffee shop, to play "Blowin in the Wind" on the music sound system.

They talked excitedly as if they had known each other for years or as close sisters, and their discussions usually returned to men in general and the number of men they have dated. Suzanne corrected Jennie, saying, "not dated — slept with." Jennie added, "What's the difference?" and they both laughed. The late 60's and early 70's was the era of love-ins, but they stayed clear of emotional entanglements. Jennie confided that she has only been with three men in any significant capacity.

Suzanne said, her eyes wide, "You are almost thirty years old and have only been with three men! You need to date more, figure out who is best for you, and most of all, have a little fun."

They talked until the student waitress in tight jeans cleared the last table, and Brian directed them to the door before locking it. One would get the impression they didn't have homes to go to.

Suzanne was tall and attractive with long, natural curly chestnut-red hair and dark eyes, and she is outspoken and a little "spacey" at times. When they first met her hair was streaked with green and blue sprayed for a garish but trendy look. She said she did drugs like everybody else, but "fortunately drugs came on the scene a little late for us to really get into them." Like others in her crowd, she was outspoken in her support for the civil-rights movement, and she was an active participant in anti-war demonstrations protesting the use of Dow Chemical's Agent Orange in Vietnam. She has a tattoo on her ankle, and she volunteered that she has another tattoo that only her boyfriends see. She is a gifted writer and is extremely intelligent. Though her attitude is a leftover of the free love and free speech movement, Jennie enjoyed her company, and they became fast friends. Jennie, herself, joined the "freaks," and embraced the 1960's counterculture lifestyle when she was in college, but her ideals changed when she had to join the work force. Her outlook on life changed; if she wanted to be successful, she had to think and dress for success.

Suzanne lived in student housing near the school, in a home with lots of bedrooms and loud music that sounded like fifty pinball machines going at once. Jennie asked her, "How can you sleep there?" "You get used to it!" She quipped.

The creative writing class was a mixed group with diverse interests, and each evening at seven they gathered around a round table presided over by Professor Tom Baird. Baird was in his forties, of medium height and stocky build. He had long sideburns a la Elvis, and his everyday attire consisted of a turtleneck sweater with a nondescript grey tweed sport coat. But he had a wonderful voice, and he mesmerized the class when reading aloud. As Jennie related to her friends, "We analyzed Bellow, Updike, Lardner, Oates and others. Professor Baird told us our reading was as important as our writing, that the two are inseparable. Then we shared our own writing with the class for their critique. At first we were shy about being the first to expose our fictional thoughts, but it soon became "old hat" and everyone was eager to "go first."

Suzanne's interest was poetry, and she credited Cervantes for that (even though he was not renowned as a poet). Her fascination was literary magazines which she referred to as "lit mags." She had been acquiring and collecting them for sometime. "I have a ton of lit mags," and she asked "Maybe I should start submitting to these journals. What do you think?"

"I would start with the smaller magazines," Jennie replied.

Professor Baird encouraged his students to send out stories or poems so they would get the taste of rejection. It seems a bit cruel, but he said they would become better writers because of rejection. He once told them, "I'm not going to teach you how to write. I'm going to teach you to look at what you have written and determine whether it is publishable."

Suzanne submitted three poems which the class thought were strong contenders, but each was returned with the usual form rejection slip. Jennie sent out a short story which Professor Baird said she might have success with, but it came right back to her. As consolation, he told them that Scott Fitzgerald had a wall papered with rejection slips, and volunteered, "Sometimes getting your work published takes more work than writing it."

Finally Suzanne got lucky; she entered a contest sponsored by Poetry Magazine, a prestigious publication considered to be a "big time" publication, and she won the award and its prize of $5,000. Her luck didn't stop there; she hit it big with two scholarly quarterlies. She was turning out work of consistent high quality. Suzanne was in the door, but Jennie was still standing outside. Professor Baird assured her that her time would come.

One night at the coffee house, Jennie was feeling despondent and confided to Suzanne that she was still having difficulty dealing with Steve's death. She woke at night from nightmares and was unable to go back to sleep. In her dreams, she saw Steve lying in a pool of blood, and she woke up screaming.

Suzanne said, "You might think this is bizarre, but if you wrote a memoir about your lives together and Steve's death, it might help to bring closure. I read a story about a person with a similar problem, and writing and putting the events and feelings on paper helped that person come to terms with death." "Please try it." Jennie agreed that it might help her.

At first, Jennie thought, "I can't write a memoir, it's too personal," but then she started writing and the words came easy. All her feelings for Steve poured from her heart. Sometimes she was crying while writing. She became so absorbed with her story that when she went to bed only her body rested; her mind continued to think and write. The manuscript which she had titled, "Steve & Me," began as a narrative of their lives together and, after his death, it became a long letter to him reminiscing about their pleasures in life, the good times and the sorrows they shared, her feelings for him then and her feelings for him now. She ended it saying, "The good times we had together will stay with me forever. I love you, I love you." It was in a way a final good-bye to Steve.

After Suzanne read it, she told Jennie it was one of the most beautiful stories she has read. She urged her to show it to Professor Baird, and he commented, "This is brilliant writing. If you would like to submit it for publication, I am certain it would be accepted. I think any publishing company would want to publish it as a book. It has all the qualities of a first-rate memoir plus it's a passionate love story and a wonderful tribute to Steve."

"The story is all that remains of our lives together, and I don't think I want to make our lives public."

"Well, it could be submitted as fiction, but you should not deprive yourself the acclaim of writing a beautiful memoir," he replied.

Jennie thought about it and decided to have it published as a memoir. She was anxious to be published even if it met telling the world her life history. Others do it, why shouldn't I? First of all, she needs to find an agent. She is about to learn firsthand the publishing business

Chapter Four

Jennie and Suzanne started life in similar circumstances both being only children born late in their mother's life, but that is where the similarity ended. Even though they grew up under different circumstances, they felt like sisters. Suzanne came from wealth, and Jennie was from a typical medium class family. Now they are equals – students aspiring to become successful writers.

Suzanne was born late in her parent's lives. Her mother had three miscarriages, and they had given up on having a child. So when she became pregnant at age 42, it was surprising to say the least. Her mother followed the doctor's orders to avoid another miscarriage, and nine months later she gave birth to a perfectly healthy baby girl.

Suzanne had a normal childhood growing up in Lake Forest; she went to Hebrew School and had her bat mitzvah at age thirteen. She had always been an impulsive, mischievous child so her parents weren't too shocked at what happened at her bat mitzvah party.

Suzanne and two girlfriends ordered banana-pineapple smoothies from the bar that was set up for guests, and then they went to a secluded area and spiked their drinks with bourbon that Suzanne had hidden in a small bottle in her large purse. They repeated this three times, and when Suzanne followed a boy to the dance floor, she promptly fell on her face. Her parents took her home and put her in bed to sleep it off.

She went east to Smith College and found her courses challenging. Smith breeds strong, independent young women, and Suzanne fit in well. She received her B.A. and then went to New York City for a career in marketing at Macy's. She always had a desire to write, so she returned to Chicago to study creative writing at Columbia, and that is where she and Jennie met.

Jennie was also born late in her parent's lives. Her mother taught school, and they had hoped to have children, but as time went on it seemed they would be childless. Finally, when her mother turned 40, she became pregnant. Even at that stage in life, her parents were ecstatic, and they doted on Jennie.

Her father worked for an engineering firm that designed and built wastewater treatment plants throughout the U.S., and he traveled extensively. This meant that her mother did most of the parenting, and they bonded early.

Jennie was a typical small town girl who lived in the same house all her life. She made friends easily but remained close to Lynn, and they were faithful friends all through school. She went to the University of Illinois at the Urbana-Champaign campus so she didn't travel far from home.

When Jennie graduated from college she left Quincy and came to Chicago to work. Like her father, she worked for an engineering company. Her father died unexpectedly of a heart attack when she was 22 years old. Her mother mourned his death and did not like being alone, so Jennie tried to get home often to be with her mother. Then her mother was offered a job at the Senior Citizen's Center, and when she wasn't working, she played bridge and 500. She made friends quickly, and she no longer complained of loneliness.

Jennie dated fairly often but didn't become enamored with anyone until she met Steve Hollis. They were crazy about each other and became inseparable. They lived in the upscale Lincoln Park neighborhood on Chicago's north side, and they fit in well with the other up-and-coming young professionals in the area. She doesn't own a car because she didn't need a car with Steve in her life. She is a design engineer at Bradley Engineering whose offices are easily accessible by bus in downtown Chicago.

Professor Baird had given Jennie a list of agents to contact, and after calling several firms she decided the Matt Shapiro Agency would best represent her work. Professor Baird was acquainted with the Matt Shapiro Agency and their success as literary agents, and he highly recommended them. Jennie sent a query letter and synopsis and waited for a reply. Mr. Baird told her that agents reject work just as publications do so be prepared to contact several agents before making a connection. Naturally, his prompt reply and request for an interview was a surprise. She was also told that memoirs sell well today, and that may explain his keen interest. Somewhere she read that a writer's relationship with her agent was just like a marriage, for better or worse, so choose wisely. Why were all those thoughts running through her mind? All she has to do is call and set up an appointment with Matt Shapiro.

The phone rang, and a pleasant voice answered, "Matt Shapiro Agency."

"I'm calling to schedule an interview with Mr. Shapiro," replied Jennie.

"I can schedule that for you – will Thursday, Jan. 24th at 1 o'clock be okay?"

"Yes, that will be fine, I'll be there."

Matt Shapiro's office was in the old Monadnock Bldg. on Jackson Blvd. in downtown Chicago. In 1893 when it was built, it was the world's largest office building. It stood only seventeen stories high, and if it wasn't listed on the National Register of Historic Places, it probably would have been demolished for a taller skyscraper.

Jennie was impressed with the building's distinguished original oak and glass entrances to each office, and it was exactly one o'clock when she opened the frosted glass door with the name "Matt Shapiro Agency" boldly etched in black. When she entered, a tall, thin man with boyishly thick brown hair and wearing dark-rimmed glasses was talking on the phone, and he spun around to face her when he heard the door open. He had a surprised look on his face, and she wondered why.

"May I help you," he asked as he greeted her.

"I'm Jennie Rogers, and I have an appointment with Mr. Shapiro."

"I'm Matt Shapiro; it's a pleasure to meet you," he said as he discreetly slipped into his sport coat, and then extended his hand in a firm handshake. "Your synopsis interests me, and I would like to read your entire manuscript," as he led her into his office, further stating, "Sometimes a memoir can be difficult to sell. Some publishers say that if the subject isn't a famous, well-known person, the writing has to be exceptional. But overall, publishers continue to snap up memoirs because they want wonderful stories about real people that are well written; those stories will always sell. Your synopsis fits that description."

After those comments, it was with some reluctance that Jennie handed him the large brown envelope. She told him she was taking creative writing at Columbia, and her instructor encouraged her to submit it for publication.

"Well, I'm certain it's well written, Columbia is known for turning out successful writers."

He paused for a moment and shuffled some papers around as the thundering Blue Line El rattled and rumbled on clattering tracks by his window. The filthy windows obscured all but the noise of the train as it streaked by. Obviously annoyed, he raised his eyebrows, and apologetically grumbled, "The rent's reasonable." While he was stacking papers, Jennie's gaze shifted to a huge gray Underwood manual typewriter on a stand next to his desk, and she imagined seeing Ernest Hemingway at work typing, "The Old Man and the Sea."

"My parents gave that to me for my bar mitzvah, and it's been a true friend all these years. I used it to write my three novels."

"You are a writer?"

"I was, but the more I got to know my agent, the more I wanted to have his job. I was tired of being tied to my desk every day staring at a piece of paper. I wanted to go a step further; I wanted to find the best talent and publish the best books."

The train had passed, and Matt went on to discuss his role as a literary agent, his fee of fifteen percent of all money earned should he be able to sell it to a publisher. He further stated he would want an exclusive and asked if she had submitted her book to another agent. Jennie replied that she had not made multiple submissions.

He told her he would like to meet with her again after he has read the manuscript and said he would call her. As he was escorting her to the door he commented, "From your synopsis, I was expecting to see an older woman with more experience." Not knowing how to comment on that remark, she simply smiled and told him she looked forward to hearing from him.

Suzanne was anxious to hear the outcome of Jennie's meeting with Matt Shapiro, so they went to The Quorum as usual after class.

Jennie eagerly stated, "I envisioned an agent's office to be a well-appointed office sitting at the top of a stately skyscraper in literary luxury, not a second floor cluttered office with the elevated tracks running by the window. I'm not kidding, the Blue Line El rumbled past, and the noise was ghastly. Matt sheepishly mumbled something about cheap rent; I know he was embarrassed. There were stacks and stacks of paper and notes everywhere, a real mess."

"Maybe he is just starting out – did he tell you how long he has been in business?

"Yes, he mentioned six and a half years and said he wouldn't want to be doing anything else. I do like him, and I think he will do a good job with my book. He asked to read my entire manuscript, so I'm anxious to hear his comments."

"His desire to read your complete manuscript means he is very interested – I think you have a winner!"

"I sure hope so, but I'm not going to sit by the phone and go nuts whenever it rings. Steve's marker is in place now, and I'm anxious to visit his grave so I'm going to Phoenix for the weekend. I called his parents, and they want me to stay with them. I'll be back for Monday evening's class."

Grace Hollis took her to the cemetery, and Jennie was surprised at its beauty. It was like a refuge or an oasis in the desert with flowers of every color adorning the headstones. They walked across the cemetery lawn past headstones drab from age until they came to the newly-placed, glossy gray slab engraved as follows: Steven R. Hollis, April 7, 1944 and February 19, 1972. She placed a single red rose on his grave marker. Wiping tears from her eyes, she dropped to her knees and told him how very much she loved him and missed him. She hoped this last good-bye will help to bring closure to his death.

Grace told her they had purchased a family plot and in time there would be a trio of gray granite rectangular markers with the name, Hollis, inscribed in black.

During the following weeks when Jennie returned home from work she would immediately check her message machine, but there was nothing from Matt Shapiro. She wasn't surprised; Professor Baird told her to expect to wait two or three weeks. "Then if you haven't heard from him, it's okay to follow-up with a phone call."

Returning home from work on a Monday, she barely got inside the door when her phone rang. It was Matt Shapiro calling to set up an appointment to discuss the publication of her book. She immediately called Suzanne and told her the news. Suzanne detected a note of sadness in her voice even though she was trying to be upbeat, and commented, "You should be bubbling over with happiness."

"I am, I truly am, but I've been thinking about Steve all day. It's February 19th, and it has been a year today. I just can't shake the doldrums." It had begun to snow, and she said, "I think I'll take a walk in the snow. Steve and I loved to walk in the snow."

"Would you like some company?"

"Suz, I would love your company."

The night was warm, and large heavy snowflakes danced in the breeze and fluttered to the ground. They walked along in darkness not seeing the snow, but feeling it on their faces until they reached the end of the block where the street lights illuminated the falling, glistening snow. Suzanne listened while Jennie reminisced about Steve. She encouraged her to talk about him knowing that was what she needed to do.

Remorsefully, Jennie said, "I really feel that Steve would be alive today if he had gone with me to the reunion. I was terribly naïve to think the reunion was going to be exciting, and I needed to be there without Steve to enjoy my high school friends and relive those carefree times. I was the only single person there, and I felt so out of place and wished Steve was with me."

"You shouldn't think that way and blame yourself for Steve's death. It was natural to be excited about the reunion and seeing your friends.

Steve would have taken that job and done what he did even if he had gone to the reunion. There's no way you should have guilty feelings over what Steve did. As you say, he liked excitement and adventure, and he acted on his own."

"Yes, Suz, I know you are right. I just can't believe Steve who was so young, so full of life and with so much to live for, is gone."

The snow began to thicken and several inches had already accumulated as they were returning to Jennie's apartment.

"I feel much better now. Let's have some coffee. Even though a year has gone by, I still feel sad and lost whenever I think of him. At first the grief was terrible, but I lived through it, and now I know there's nothing wrong with suffering; its part of the grieving process. I don't want to forget him, and I know I never will, but I have to be able to live with his senseless murder. I wish I knew the whole story – I want to know why Steve became involved with real estate fraud and why he agreed to do everything he was asked to do. I'll admit he was not your average CPA— he had an adventurous side, and being a part of the FBI's investigations would appeal to his venturesome spirit. Did he decide to become involved just for the excitement of it all?"

Chapter Five

Matt welcomed Jennie into his office stating, "I started reading it and immediately just loved it. I gave it to my associate to read, and she agreed, "We have to have this book."

He drew up a chair opposite his desk which was covered with stacks of paper that appeared to be manuscripts. He hastily tried to rearrange the stacks, then patted his jacket pocket feeling for the pen that he habitually misplaced, while stating, "You grabbed the reader right away and held their interest with the wonderful way you tell a story. Editors have little patience. If the first page doesn't grab them, it goes to the slush pile. You have a strong voice, and your story starts on Page one. It's so common for beginning writers to ramble on and not start their story until Page ten, and by that time the reader has left them. Most people only read two or three pages of a book when looking for a book to buy; some make their decision based upon the first page. But, more important, there aren't any clichés – if I see a cliché, its out!" and for further emphasis, he punctuated his words with a click of his ballpoint pen.

He went on to tell her he had sent her manuscript to an editor at Harper Jones Publishing Company, and the editor said, "We can make this a best seller, but I want a revision."

"The editor pointed out that you are dedicating the book to your classmate and published poet, Suzanne Stein, whose consolation and friendship in your time of grief sustained you, and her encouragement in writing made this book possible. The editor wants to know more about Suzanne's abiding friendship and encouragement in writing the book. He thinks her role in your life would add further human interest to the story. The indication that she is a published poet is also of interest. He may see her as a potential client."

"I would like to meet with you and Suzanne as soon as possible so we can work on the revision. Would Saturday at 9 a.m. be okay?"

"Yes, that will be fine unless it's a problem with Suzanne. If it is, I'll get back to you."

When Jennie told Suzanne the editor wanted to know about her and her role in writing the book, in her usual nonchalant, witty manner, she said, "Tell him I was born in Lake Forest, the only child of alcoholic parents," and she went on to say:

"The other day my tipsy mother fell on the ice and refused to let me take her to the doctor. It was a bad fall; she has one black-and-blue butt cheek and a white one." She said, "Its all right, dear, a glass of sherry will ease the pain."

"My father, who is president of an injection molding company, can actually set down his gin and tonic long enough to eat dinner. Throughout the meal, he expounds on injection molding. I still don't know anything about it."

Jennie laughed and said, "I'll let you tell Matt your life story; don't forget to bring along the awards and tributes you've received for your poetry. They may want to publish a book of your poems. What would you do after your fame and fortune?"

Suzanne thought a moment and said, "I have always wanted to drive across the country. I would ignore the utter boredom of Iowa and Nebraska, sip a Bud with a cowboy in Colorado, listen to Bruce Springsteen croon "Born to Run" at 3 o'clock in the morning in Las Vegas, and chat with strangers at gas stations along Route 66. In other words, see our magnificent country. What would you do?"

"I guess I'd do the same. Take a long or permanent vacation from my job and travel, but I want to see the world. I'd like to lose myself on a sunny, white-sand beach on a Caribbean island, stroll the streets of Paris, and cruise the Mediterranean."

"You better start your second book," replied Suzanne.

Jennie and Suzanne arrived at Shapiro's office on time, eager to learn the publishing business and what their role would be during publication. Since it was Saturday, Matt Shapiro had abandoned his sport coat and tie for slacks and a sweater which added to his good looks. Suzanne nudged Jennie and whispered, "You know how to pick em."

Momentarily, Matt seemed a little nervous having two attractive young woman sitting opposite him at his desk. Suzanne's instantly likable manner put him at ease, and the interview went well. It was obvious that he was impressed and maybe smitten with her, and Suzanne was not unapproachable. Out of the blue, she asked him, "What excites you about your job?"

He was more than a little surprised, but said in a business-like manner, "At the end of the day feeling I have done my best to get a book published for an author and actually calling the writer and saying, "your book is going to be published.""

Suzanne is not shy. "I like that" she stated.

Matt informed them that after publication they should be willing to do everything they can to help in the sales. He said they should go to bookstores, promote the book, and be available for book signings. Give up a few weekends to sell yourself and your book. Tell everybody you know and don't know about the book. Be willing and available to travel to bookstores out of the area and out of state. You put a lot of work into the book; make it pay off.

He continued, "My favorite client is a gifted writer who also understands that publishing a book is not just writing the book, but is willing to participate in the marketing of the book, getting themselves out there and using their connections to sell the book. A lot of writers are introverts who just want to be left alone to sit at their desks and write. They don't think their work is good enough, and I have to convince them they are great and that everyone will love them. I don't see that in you or Suzanne." With her eyes fixed on his face, Suzanne had been listening intently, and she nodded in agreement.

"I'll submit the revision and contact you when the publisher has made a decision."

Leaving his office, Suzanne said, "I really like him; I'm not sure if it's his shiny brown hair or the way his butt looked in his Brooks Brothers khakis."

Chapter Six

*B*ob Barnett, the editor at Harper Jones Publishing, didn't waste any time in getting back to Matt advising they had approved the revision and wanted to publish the book. Initially, they will print 10,000 copies and do their best to convince all the major bookstores to stock the book. He also told Matt they will do everything they could do to get good reviews. "Reviews do sell books," he said, "but don't be discouraged if you don't get a New York Times review. A person may not buy the book right away, but they write down the names of books that sound interesting and buy them later. We will submit reviews to all the major newspapers, including your Chicago Tribune."

Barnett called Matt requesting confirmation of the title, book size, hard or soft cover, indexing, and so forth, and he told him the design department would submit jacket and cover designs for Jennie's approval. Matt commented to Jennie, "Even though most people don't buy a book based on the book's jacket, it is the first thing they see, and an attractive jacket will tempt them to take the book off the shelf and begin reading."

They decided the biographical note inside the book cover will simply read: "Jennie Rogers was born and raised in Quincy, Illinois and was educated in its public schools. She attended the University of Illinois majoring in design engineering. She currently lives in Chicago. This is her first book-length publication."

Matt called Jennie at her office with the good news and set a date to meet and go over Barnett's request. Jennie was ecstatic, and she immediately called Suzanne.

At writing class that evening, Suzanne stepped forward and announced that Jennie's book will be published. Everyone stood and applauded vigorously. "We're all going to Tony's to celebrate – see you there."

As usual, Tony's was jammed, and there would be a wait so they went into the bar. As Jennie walked through the bar, she cautiously glanced at the booth in the corner and stood frozen, staring at the man with dark curly hair and dark eyes. The man looked away, but then again looked at Jennie staring at him. He rose, went to her and said, "Hi, I'm John Cauley – have we met?" Regaining her composure, Jennie replied, "I'm sorry, I thought you were someone else."

Suzanne rushed to her side, took her by the elbow and said, "C'mon, Jennie, we found a booth," and continued, "Jennie, there will always be someone sitting in that booth. You musn't think back to that night when Steve was there. You musn't torture yourself. Tonight we are going to celebrate your success; let's see a smile.

"Suz; what would I do without you."

Everyone raised a glass as Suzanne said, "Here's to Jennie Rogers – the first in the class to have a book published. May her success rub off on all of us." Applause and laughter followed, and Jennie said, "Thanks guys – you are a great class."

The realization of success began to sink in when she actually was faced with decisions she never expected to encounter. Jennie wanted a hard cover with jacket because it seemed to be more professional, and Matt suggested they send a photo of her to include on the back of the jacket or inside the jacket cover. He said, "A photo of the author definitely results in increased book sales." He advised against the book being indexed; it's costly and not beneficial as far as a memoir or fiction is concerned.

Matt then told her Barnett would like to change the title of the book from "Steve & Me" to **A Brief Wondrous Life.** Jennie's eyes lit up, and she wholeheartedly agreed, saying, "Yes, I like that a lot, it actually describes the book; that's perfect."

Jennie asked, "Do you think the audience of my book is stereotyped as young readers?"

"No, not at all," replied Matt, "Its written with enough humor and heart to appeal not only to young readers, but also to a mature audience. The characters aren't too wise or too perfect. No one wants to read about a person who has it all together or is perfect. That would be boring. Your book transcends all age groups and genders."

"I can't believe this is all happening and that I will wake up and find it was a dream."

"I hear what you are saying," Matt said, "For me, it didn't become reality until one day while riding the subway I saw someone actually reading my book."

"But don't stop with this book," he continued. "Don't let your talent go to waste. I will be waiting to represent your second book."

He then told her that as soon as copies are available, he would contact bookstores in the Chicago area to promote her book and arrange book signings. He further stated, "Don't fill up your weekends, you will need to be available – it's the life of an author. I don't think you and Suzanne will need me, but I'll help you get off on the right foot."

"Thanks, Matt, I appreciate your frankness.

Jennie called Steve's parents to tell them the news and promised to send them a copy as soon as she receives her advance copies. She will autograph it to Grace & Jim Hollis, loving parents of Steve Hollis.

She will ask Matt to get the book into the bookstores in Quincy and immediately envisioned the headlines in the Quincy newspaper, "Local Girl Becomes Celebrated Author." But first she has to sell it in Chicago.

When Jennie and Suzanne approached the bookstore, they were amazed to see a large colorful poster in the window advertising the book, **A Brief Wondrous Life.** Borders Books & Music on Michigan Avenue was Jennie's first signing event, and she had invited several friends to attend in case no one showed up. As she entered, they rushed to greet and congratulate her, and the feelings of apprehension left. Matt had told her a lot of first-time authors do that to avoid the panicky feeling of being stood up like the proverbial bride left at the altar.

Soon the store began to fill with people, and she looked around in awe thinking, "Wow, these people are strangers – they are here because they are interested in my book." Suzanne was answering questions and directing people to get in line. Their eyes met and Suzanne smiled and gave her the high sign. Her jitters disappeared, and she became engrossed in conversation with what seemed to be a never-ending line of people.

Jennie and Suzanne noticed a woman who had been standing and reading her book, close the cover, and throw it down, saying, "The main character is killed at the beginning of the book – why bother," and she hurried out of the store. They smiled as if to say, "She will be good fodder for a coffee gab session."

Matt surprised them when he walked in with a camera and asked Suzanne to take a picture of him with Jennie and the store manager. He winked and said, "Good publicity."

Matt suggested to Jennie that she walk around the store when not busy signing to talk to people. He said, "Most people think authors are unapproachable. Prove them wrong. Book signings are the place to be friendly. If people have the opportunity to talk to an author, they will want to buy a signed copy of the book."

Before she left, the store manager asked Jennie to sign the books they will have in stock.

When they left the bookstore it was late afternoon and getting dark. Matt said, "Anyone for coffee, I'm buying." Over coffee, Matt said he asked the cashier how many books were sold, and she said out of the twenty-four they bought, twenty-one books were sold today. "That's very good for a first book release. I think the attractive jacket design had something to do with it, and you girls were friendly and approachable. That means a lot; it leaves a great impression. You have to sell yourself to sell the book!"

It was Saturday night and Jennie and Suzanne decided to go to Tony's for dinner to rehash their first book signing. As they were being seated, Jennie walked past the corner booth without a thought. She was going to put that behind her and live for the future. They discussed Matt, the day's activities, and future book signings.

"That was the most fun I've had in months. How about you?" Jennie proclaimed.

"Yes, it was great fun. Matt definitely knows his stuff. His advice made it a success. I really like him.

Jennie went on, "Even if you don't sell many books, you meet interesting people. And, there's always the possibility they will buy it later."

"I definitely want a book sign in Quincy. I want everybody to know that a local girl made a name for herself in the literary world, even though the book is just a memoir. Am I a little ahead of myself? After all, the book could bomb."

"Well, that's true, Jennie. The book hasn't been out long enough to go to the top of the best seller list at the New York Times. Let's go to

Quincy and sell it, to get an idea how it will sell in small town, USA."

"I'll ask Matt to send a press release to the Herald and contact Waldenbooks. Even though I don't know anyone at the bookstore personally, being from Quincy will help me get my foot in the door, I hope."

Sunday morning dawned bright and sunny, and Jennie settled in her favorite cushy chair with a mug of coffee and the Chicago Tribune. Matt had told her he submitted a press release on her book, and she flicked through all the glitzy ads, the sports and travel sections until she found the entertainment section. Leafing through page after page of the movie section, she found the best book seller list. **"A Brief Wondrous Life"** wasn't listed, but next to it under "New Titles" was a press release stating:

"New from Harper Jones Publishing: **A Brief Wondrous Life**," A Poignant and Compelling Memoir, written by Jennie Rogers, a New and Wonderfully-Gifted Writer. Now Available at Leading Bookstores."

She sat, reading it over and over, savoring every word and thinking back to the day she started writing **"A Brief Wondrous Life**." What she envisioned as a painful, solitary experience, is turning out to be the most fascinating endeavor of her life.

Now she will put her heart into promoting and selling her book.

Chapter Seven

It was Monday morning, and Jennie called Matt to discuss a book sign in Quincy. She wanted the sign to take place on a Saturday at Waldenbooks, the largest bookstore in town. Matt said he was happy to hear she wanted to go out of town with the book, and he would send a press release to the Quincy Herald.

The News Release that Matt submitted to the Quincy Herald read:

"For Immediate Release: Matt Shapiro Agency announces a book launch by local author, Jennie Rogers. A former Quincy native is launching her new book entitled, **"A Brief Wondrous Life**," a poignant and compelling memoir just released by Harper Jones Publishing Co. Jennie Rogers, a new and talented writer, is entering the literary world with a book that is expected to be on everyone's best seller list. The public is invited to a book signing at Waldenbooks on Sat., March 16, at 1 p.m."

Jennie called her friend, Lynn, and asked, "Did you see my news release in the Herald? Are you going to be there?"

"I certainly did; I wouldn't miss it. I'll invite everyone I know to the book signing. I'm so happy for you."

Jennie wanted this book sign to be her biggest and most successful. Matt said he would have 50 books shipped to the store. Every detail will be taken care of in advance. The bookstore indicated they usually have the local radio station publicize their event.

The weekend finally arrived, and Friday night after work, Suzanne picked up Jennie at her apartment for the drive to Quincy. Sliding into her Buick, Jennie said, "Suz, I owe you – Big Time." Suz smiled and said, "I'll remember that, Jen."

Driving along the country roads burned white from highway department salt, Jennie told her all about growing up in Quincy, her friend, Lynn, and other friends who still call it home. Jennie and Suzanne were planning to stay over on Saturday night and drive back on Sunday.

Soon the city lights appeared in the distance, and they were passing Burma-Shave signs, the car lots with their colorful pennants snapping in the wind, tractor sales, and feed stores, the usual assorted businesses on the edge of town. Jennie began chattering out of nervousness wondering if anyone would be interested enough to actually attend the "sign" besides Lynn and her mother.

"Don't worry about it, Jen. I'm certain Matt will have every detail taken care of. That's his job, and he's good at it. I wonder if he will stay over tomorrow night."

The bell above the door tinkled as they entered the Waldenbooks store in the shopping mall, and there was a handsome young man shelving books in the nearly empty store. Jennie went up to him asking to see the manager. She wasn't expecting the impossibly handsome man who looked more like a famous sports figure to say, "I'm the manager – John Gardner. Are you Jennie Rogers?"

Yes, and this is my friend, Suzanne Stein. We stopped in to see if there is anything we can help you with."

"Well, yes there is. Where do you want to have your table placed? I was just going to put some posters in the window and place books around the store. Maybe you would like to help with that."

"Yes, I would like to set up displays of my book. I love your store, the smell of printer's ink and the eye-catching displays of colorful glossy jackets. The atmosphere is so inviting."

"Thank you, I like to create a place where people will want to browse and stay awhile. We serve coffee and often have snacks. We have good traffic, and I try to host good events to keep things interesting. We host reading groups and have author readings and signings, to name a few. I hope you will like what we have planned for today."

Jennie and Suzanne walked around the store setting up displays and locating the table. Jennie told John she wouldn't be sitting at the table unless she is signing a book. She prefered to walk around and greet customers and talk to them.

He commented, "You have done this before," and Jennie nodded as though she has had ten signings instead of one. Suzanne looked at her and winked.

As they were leaving, John told them, "We have a bunch of balloons to put outside the door so it will be easier for people to find us. Also, someone from the radio station will be here to interview you, and we have arranged for a guitarist who is a local personality to sit in the corner and play and sing a few numbers. He won't be obtrusive or loud; his music will be low-key background music, yet enjoyable. He has a great following here in Quincy. I know you will like him; He will be a big draw. It will be a big event."

"Thank you, John, it sounds great. I really appreciate everything you are doing for me – I hope we sell lots of books for you."

At that moment, the door opened and Matt appeared. After greetings, he asked John if he had someone to help carry a couple of boxes of books from his car into the store. "I had the feeling that the shipment of 50 books wouldn't be enough so I brought 50 more with me today. After the books were unloaded, Jennie asked him to accompany her and Suzanne to her home for lunch. Matt replied he would love to.

Driving up to the store, they were greeted with colorful balloons, the radio station truck, and an early crowd of people. Jennie thought, "I can't believe this is all for me – it's like a dream." Upon entering, Lynn and Roger Smith rushed to greet her, and they introduced her to a group of people waiting to see and talk to her. Seeing Lynn put Jennie at ease, and she looked around for other familiar faces.

Without warning, a man from KTOV radio shoved a microphone in her face and asked if he could ask her a few questions. Jennie smiled and said that would be okay:

"How does it feel knowing that people are buying your book?"

"Very flattering. Especially when someone says how much they enjoyed it because at the time, I was writing it for myself and didn't think others would be interested."

"How long have you been writing?"

"For several years, but I began writing in earnest a year ago when I enrolled in creative writing at Columbia."

"What was your initial reaction to the book?

"Wow, did I write that! When you haven't read your written material for a long time, it is new and surprising."

"Do you have any advice for beginning writers?"

"Yes, take a course or join a writing group where assignments are given so that you are forced to write."

"Thank you, and I wish you much success," he replied.

Matt had been standing behind her, and he commented, "That was a good interview, Jennie, you gave all the right answers."

It seemed as though everyone began picking up copies of the book, and Matt and Suzanne started a line to Jennie's table, and she went to work personalizing and signing them. The store filled up and a crowd of people mingled around her. Jennie could hear the guitarist quietly playing "Blowin in the Wind." She smiled knowingly and looked around for Suzanne. She was locked in Matt's embrace, and Jennie wondered what brought that on.

John appeared at her side asking if there was anything he could do for her. Jennie smiled and whispered, "Yes, pick up a pen and help me." He laughed and said, "You're doing great." Quietly, she thought "I must have signed a hundred books already."

The store was definitely taking on a party atmosphere. Suzanne remarked to Matt, "This is so cool!"

As the day wore on, the crowds thinned, and the store was nearing closing time. Matt and John were busy going through sales receipts and the inventory of books left. Matt said, "If we sell these remaining six books, it will be a sellout!" John said he would order an additional 24 books to have in stock. "Many times people just come to the "sign" for the entertainment but come back later and buy a book."

Jennie finally had a chance to chat with Suzanne: "It seems that every time I turned to look for you, Matt was hugging you."

"Isn't that great – the first time it happened was when I asked the guitarist to play "Blowin in the Wind." He is a Bob Dylan fan, too. Later I told him Cervantes was the inspiration for my poetry. He couldn't believe it because he thinks Don Quixote is the world's greatest novel. Can you believe that our thoughts run along the same wave link? Is this destiny, or what?"

In an offhand manner, Suzanne commented that John was not a bad looking guy, and asked "Did you notice his fingers – the only ring he is wearing is a class ring and it appears to be a college ring."

"I didn't look at his hands,"

"Jennie, you are single and well past 21; that should be the first thing you see in a guy."

"Suz, I'm not so old that I'm desperate. If I see a guy who appeals to me, then I will check him for rings."

"Okay, you do it your way. Matt wants to take us someplace for a celebration dinner, and he is going to ask John to join us. Where do you suggest we go?"

"I would like to go to the Starlight – it was the hangout for high school kids, the place where I spent the better part of my teenage years. I hear they still have good food but a different clientele even though the décor hasn't changed. They probably still have the same plastic menus and the same sticky booths, but it will be fun."

"Okay, we will all relive our dorky teenage years.

Four tired but extremely happy people eagerly entered the Starlight, each savoring their own particular success. The evening may be a turning point in each of their lives:

Jennie Rogers was basking in the glow of a successful book signing event. Matt Shapiro was celebrating his success as agent to an award-winning author. John Gardner, as a purveyor of books, had just hosted a sellout book sign event. Suzanne Stein, as the author's mentor, was in a position to win the charms of her agent.

After reflecting on the events of the afternoon, their conversations turned to more personal interests. Jennie commented to John that he had the appearance of being a professional athlete, and he stated he had played amateur baseball and football during high school and college. But amateur baseball teams are becoming a thing of the past, and he grew tired of becoming beat up on the football field so he started playing golf, and that is his passion now. Turning to Jennie, he asked, "Do you play?"

"I used to play with Steve," and her voice faltered and broke. John took her hand in his saying, "Its okay, I read your book, you and Steve did everything together, I understand." The soft, comforting touch of his hand enabled her to regain her composure, and she continued, "I played to keep him company when he had no one else. I like the game, but was never good enough to really enjoy it. Steve was a five handicap, he was very good."

The Starlight had the appearance of a diner during the Sixties, and Matt discovered the jukebox. Soon the strains of "Blowin in the Wind" could be heard, and he led Suzanne to the dance floor. Jennie thought to herself, "I think that song will forever be etched in my brain." John said, "Let's dance" and led her to the floor.

When the evening came to a close, John commented, "I go to Chicago occasionally to visit friends and see a Cubs or Bears game, could I call you?" Jennie said she would like that and gave him her phone number.

Before saying goodnight, Suzanne said, "This has been the best day of my life."

Jennie agreed, "It was a very good day."

Jennie and Suzanne had a lot to talk about on their drive back to Chicago. They got a late start because Jennie's mother tried every ploy she knew to keep them with her longer. Jennie realized her mother was lonely and admitted her guilt in not coming home more often.

When they finally turned on the highway heading north, it was mid-afternoon, and they settled back for a 4-hour drive. Jennie broke the silence. "So what do you know about Matt – is he married, divorced, or what?"

Suzanne replied, "I think he is divorced; he didn't say so and I didn't ask, but I remember when we went to his office. The first thing I look for is pictures of children or any sign of martial life. There wasn't anything of that nature in his office. If a man is divorced, he doesn't have pictures of his children around because an attractive female client would be discouraged, and it would be difficult for him to pursue her. So, he gets rid of the evidence."

Jennie couldn't stop laughing saying, "Suz, you are something else."

"Well," Suz replied, "I've read about those things, and it eliminates a lot of guesswork. Incidentally, he asked for my phone number so I'll find out soon. What's with you and John?"

Jennie said, "He asked for my phone number and said he occasionally gets to Chicago. That doesn't sound like he is very anxious to see me, does it?"

Chapter Eight

"Thanks, everyone, you guys really are the best," Jennie said as she hugged each person standing in a circle around her. She had just blown out the candles on her birthday cake that was covered with so many candles they almost toppled off the cake's sides. Jennie remarked, "Am I really that old!" After devouring the cake, they went to her apartment for a champagne toast before heading to Tony's.

They had just stepped inside Jennie's apartment when her phone rang. She hurriedly answered it and a male voice said, "Hi, Jennie, this is John Gardner. I just wanted to call and see if you'll have dinner with me tonight?"

Surprised, Jennie ventured, "Dinner? Tonight?"

"You probably have plans, don't you? I'm sorry to call at the last minute."

"Well, yes, as a matter of fact it's my birthday, and my classmates are treating me to dinner at Tony's."

"Happy birthday, can we celebrate it at dinner tomorrow night?"

"Yes, I would like that, John," and she quickly hung up as if she was afraid he might change his mind.

Suzanne said, "Don't say a word. I can tell from the way your eyes lit up, it was John, wasn't it? He didn't waste time – it was just two weeks ago when we were in Quincy."

Opening the champagne, Jennie said, "Yes, I thought it was just small talk when he said he occasionally gets to Chicago."

Suzanne and the other girls toasted her 29th birthday and added, "And here's to Jennie and John." Suz said, "I think it is definitely fate that he decided to call you on your birthday; a sign that you are destined to be together forever."

The next day Jennie left the office on time and raced to the beauty shop for a manicure and hair style. She went through her closet and assembled various outfits, finally deciding on a skirt that just skimmed her knees and a beige cashmere cardigan that revealed just the right amount of cleavage.

When she greeted John at the door, he smelled both soapy and minty when he leaned forward to give her a peck on the cheek.

"It's really great to see you, Jennie," he said as he took her hand and led her out into the hallway.

They went to a neighborhood Italian restaurant, and John expertly ordered a choice Syrah. Jennie likes red wines, and she was impressed with his knowledge of the wine list.

"I had a feeling you are an Aries," he said after toasting her birthday. "You have all the traits of someone born under the fire sign; you are confident, ambitious and creative. And, you are courageous and not afraid to take on any project that interests you. Also, you have shy, sensitive eyes that reveal a need to be loved."

Jennie thought to herself, "Wow, you know what every girl wants to hear,"

He went on, "Tell me, what have you been doing, are you writing, have you started a second book?"

"Aside from class assignments, I haven't been writing, but I've thought it would be fun to write a romance novel and sell it to Harlequin. Did you know they are the No. 1 sellers of romance novels?"

John laughed and said, "Yes, I should know! Romance novels have a great following, even among men! I think you would be good at that," and, then softly commented, "If your heroine ever gets into a dilemma, let me know – maybe I can help you." Then in a serious tone, he said, "But I'm forgetting the good news; all of your books have been sold, and I have reordered again."

"I have good news, too," Jennie said. "Matt told me Harper Jones will soon be making their first quarterly royalty payment of $10,000. Of course, Matt gets 15% of that. When this semester ends, Suzanne and I may take a trip somewhere. We are trying to decide what to do – take a cruise or travel someplace here."

"I'm planning a trip to San Francisco and Tiburon this summer," John replied. "I love to go to the waterfront and eat on the dock in back of Sam's Café in Tiburon. The food is great and the scenery is gorgeous. Boaters literally anchor and walk up the ramps to the dock to eat. Everybody is friendly; it's a fun atmosphere. Of course, you never lack for anything to do in San Francisco."

"I've never been to Tiburon; it sounds like a wonderful place. I, too, love San Francisco."

When they were saying good-night at her door, he leaned forward and feather kissed her on her neck, and she suddenly felt safe and warm all over, the way she felt with Steve. "Now why am I thinking of Steve," she thought.

The next morning, Jennie's phone rang and half asleep, she felt her way to the bedside table and fumbled for the phone. It was Suzanne, and her first words were, "Did I wake you?"

Jennie mumbled, "What time is it?"

"Its 8 o'clock, don't you have to go to work?"

"Oh my God, yes. I've got to rush, what's on your mind?"

"Well, guess what happened while you were dining with John?" Before Jennie could answer, Suz said, "Matt called, and we are going out for dinner Saturday night. Do you believe it?"

When her phone rang Sunday morning, she knew it would be Suzanne; she had too much to tell to wait any longer than a few hours.

"How was it, Suz?" Jennie asked before Suzanne had a chance to say anything.

"We had a great time, he is so cool away from the office,"

"Well, start from the beginning."

"He came up to my room in the dorm or "our dysfunctional house," as we call it, and, as usual, everyone's music player was blasting simultaneously – you know how it is - and his comment was the same as yours, "how can you sleep here?" Right away he became possessive and acted as though I was a puppy dog in the pound that needed to be rescued and given a good home. Isn't he wonderful?"

Jennie said, "I think he really cares for you."

"I can't wait until he sees my other dysfunctional home, or maybe I should avoid that – I may never see him again."

"Suz, there's nothing unusual about your parents, they enjoy life, and they care about you."

"I can hear my father now. He will welcome Matt into the family and want him to take over the injection molding business. He will take him through the plant the very first day he meets him, he's so anxious for me to marry so he will finally have a son. Mother will smile sweetly and call him, 'dear'."

"We went to *Rosebud* for dinner and first of all, I need to tell you his father, Sidney Shapiro, is a writer whose latest best seller is "The Still of the Night." Matt said he wrote, too, but right away he wanted to be an agent or an editor. He asked to see my poetry. He thinks he can sell it as a collection for a book. I was so thrilled; I told him I would drop it off at his office on Monday."

"Suz, that is just great, I'm so happy for you. It's interesting that his father writes, he didn't tell me that. Incidentally, did you find out whether he was divorced?"

"Yes, we had a candid conversation about that. Her name is Susan, and they were married for three years. Matt said she didn't want children and eventually didn't want to be married. So, they separated, and she joined the Peace Corps. She wanted to make a difference in people's lives and was sent to Honduras where she helped to build housing, furniture and even latrines for some of the poorest people in the world. Our separation was an amicable one, and we are still friends. Then he said that's enough about me, let's talk about you."

Suzanne remarked, "I was so impressed with Susan, I didn't want to talk about my run-of-the-mill life, but I told him about my years at Smith where I majored in marketing and the time I spent at Macy's in New York arranging bras in sales racks and straightening bath towel displays. All good Jewish girls put in a stint at Macy's. I began to write poetry and became bored with my job, so I returned home to Chicago and enrolled in creative writing at Columbia. I lived at home until I grew tired of excessive parental guidance. My parents didn't realize I had grown up."

"Matt said I made the right career change. He said I have a talent for writing, and I am doing the right thing by pursuing it. After reading some of my poetry, he said I am a poet capable of shouting or whispering, and singing or weeping. Isn't he great! I am going to let him try to sell it."

"That's exciting, Suz," Jennie replied, "I'll help you with your book signings or maybe we can have dual book signings. By the way, I'm going to Quincy next weekend to visit Mom. She gets very lonely."

"Oh, she will like that. Are you going to look up John?"

"No, I want to spend the short time I will have with Mother. I don't want to go there and just say hi and goodbye; I'd like to spend some quality time with her. But I will probably call Lynn and maybe we can get together with her. Lynn and I grew up together so Mother treats her like another daughter. But, in the meantime, I'm anxious to hear what Matt thinks of your poetry."

"We'll talk about it Monday night," replied Suzanne.

Chapter Nine

It was Friday, and Jennie was taking that all-too-familiar train trip to Quincy to visit her mother. She has made this trip more often than she remembers except for the trip to attend her high school reunion, and she'd like to forget that. She associates it with Steve's death, and she often wonders if their "falling out" over the reunion had something to do with Steve's sudden decision to move to Phoenix. Even though they had talked about moving there, she thought he made a hasty decision. She continued to feel guilty for not wanting him to attend her reunion, and she thought he would be alive today if he hadn't gone when he did. She wonders if she will ever learn the details surrounding his murder. She needed to know to bring closure to his death.

The sky was a flawless blue, a perfect spring day. She settled back in her seat and gazed out at a farmer planting his crop while crows swooped down behind the tractor to get their share of the grain. The little Farmall tractor moved like a snail up and down the furrows. Soon the fertile fields will be green with lush vegetation as the cycle repeats itself year after year.

Her mother idolized her since the publication of her book and constantly asked about sales. She wondered what her father's reaction would have been. She envisioned him saying, "don't give up your day job. You could end up selling toasters for a living." He would caution her that "writing one book won't make you rich and famous." (Jennie thought: is this Dad encouraging me to begin writing a second book?)

Jennie had called Lynn to tell her she was coming, and Lynn invited her and her mother for dinner Saturday night. "It will be casual," Lynn said, "Roger has begun a routine of cooking on the grill on Saturday nights. He prides himself on being a great chef and likes to show off his culinary skills on friends. Do you like ribs? He has perfected a wonderful sauce; I know you will like them."

She picked up her book, relishing some scarce reading time and before long the train slowed and came to a stop at the Quincy station. She looked out at the few people waiting, and there was her mother frantically waving to her. They embraced and walked toward the familiar blue *Chevrolet Impala* that was her father's pride and joy. He always liked a large car and bragged about how powerful it was. Jennie commented, "Mother how old is this car? I remember how Dad loved it. You really keep it in good shape."

"I think it's about 15 years old. It doesn't have a lot of miles on it because I don't drive that much nowadays."

"I'm thinking about getting a car again. Parking is awful where I live, but I'd like to be able to get around more – maybe take a vacation trip. With Steve, I didn't need a car, but now I do. I feel so restricted."

"I know what you mean. Even though I don't drive a lot, I want to be able to go where I want when I want. I'm used to being independent and so are you. What kind of a car would you get?

"I don't know yet; it has to be small for parking. Like Steve, I've always wanted to own a Mustang – but I'd like a black Mustang. I remember the old beat-up '65 hunter-green Mustang with beige top and leather seats that Steve bought with the graduation money he had put into savings to earn interest and grow. He wasn't planning to spend it on a car, but he fell in love with it at first sight, and it was fun to drive when it started. It looked great, but it was constantly in the repair shop and cost him money he didn't have, so he had to get rid of it. It broke his heart and mine – he looked so hunky driving it!

"That's an expensive car, but maybe you could get a better price here in Quincy than in the Chicago area," her mother volunteered.

"You are right, Mother, I'll check the Sunday paper and then check pricing in Chicago. I'll ask Suzanne to take me to a couple of dealers to see what they can offer."

"If you would like, I could take you to a Ford dealer here tomorrow."

"Okay, let's do that. Now I'm anxious to find out what they sell for today and what kind of a deal I can get. Thanks, Mom."

Saturday afternoon they drove to a Ford dealer in the area, and Jennie commented, "This is the last thing I expected to do this weekend."

"I'm happy you are considering getting a car; you will have more freedom, and maybe I'll see you more often," her mother said, slyly glancing at Jennie for her reaction.

"It's a good possibility, that train trip is getting very boring."

Jennie's eyes lit up at seeing the black Mustang of her dreams, but seeing the basic price tag of $20,000 with no additions, she gulped. "I'd have to sell a ton of books to afford that."

Driving up the driveway, Jennie knew they were in for a treat. Roger's barbeque smelled spicy and hot. Her mother remarked, "I wasn't particularly hungry until now!"

While enjoying a glass of wine, Lynn asked Jennie if she had stopped at the bookstore.

"No, I didn't. Mother and I had other things to do."

"Well, I stopped by and I saw that they are still promoting your book. I didn't talk to John as he was busy."

"Oh," Jennie asked, "What do you know about him or what do you think of him?

"He's good looking, his wife teaches school, he's about our age."

Jennie gasped in surprise, "Are you serious?

"Serious about what – his good looks?"

Jennie lamely commented, "I didn't know his wife taught school." Stunned and desperate to change the subject, she blurted out, "I'm going to buy a new car."

Roger's ears perked up at the mention of a "new car," and after much discussion that continued into dinner, he suggested she look at a Pontiac Grand Prix.

The evening proceeded on a positive note, and Jennie was dying to get back to Chicago to tell Suzanne about John so she could either laugh or cry. The more she thought about it, the more she just wanted to have a good laugh with Suz.

Boarding the train on Sunday, Jennie hugged her mother and vowed to return soon. "Maybe I'll drive next time."

Jennie's train arrived at 6:30, and she was going to meet Suzanne at Tony's at 7. After they were seated and placed their orders, Jennie said, "Suz, would you believe that John is married!"

"What a creep – how did you find out?"

"It was just a casual remark," Jennie replied, "Lynn commented that his wife teaches school. I was terribly shocked and didn't want any further conversation on the subject, so I awkwardly changed the subject. It was embarrassing to say the least, and I was really hurt. I had thought that John and I had something wonderful going, he's fun to be with, and I really like him."

"What are you going to say if he calls again?"

"I'll just tell him I don't go out with married men."

Suz replied, "I can hear it now, she doesn't understand me."

"Well, I don't care what he says, I'm not interested. Incidentally that disproves your theory on rings. My only interest now is cars — I've decided to buy a car so I can be independent and not have to rely on my friends for transportation; will you help me — will you once again be my chauffeur?"

"I would love that, I like to shop for cars especially when someone else is buying."

It didn't take long for Jennie to decide on a car. Roger's eloquent sales pitch on a Grand Prix left a vivid impression so she decided to check it out. She liked its quality and operating features, and it came in black. Now she felt she was finally "letting it go and getting on with life."

Chapter Ten

ennie's book continued to sell well, and Suzanne was working with Matt on getting her poetry together for publication in book form. This activity and writing class were encouraging Jennie to start her second book. Needing some encouragement, she turned to Matt, who jokingly said, "Tell people you are writing a book, that way you can't back out easily." This book will be fiction, and he reminded her that most fiction is written to entertain, and she should keep that in mind. She began thinking up a plot and preparing an outline, and soon she was engrossed in her second book.

When she was well into her book, she commented to Suzanne, "I sometimes wonder how long I can continue to hold a day job and write when I wake and get my best ideas in the middle of the night. I have to keep a yellow pad and pencil on the bedside table. Writing dialogue is difficult yet I know it is essential to a story."

Suzanne laughed and told her "My secret for writing dialogue is to talk to myself when in traffic jams or in the shower so as to get used to having internal dialogue. Just be careful to do it when you are alone."

"Why do we write when in reality, we suffer while doing so? Do the rewards compensate for the suffering?"

"Your first book certainly sold well."

Jennie's turning point in life occurred when Steve was killed, and she took up writing as her way to achieve independence. A few weeks later Suzanne was experiencing her turning point; a situation that would change her life dramatically. Her father had suffered a debilitating stroke which left him with paralysis of his right side, and he was unable to speak coherently. The doctors told her that with therapy and treatment, he would recover, but probably not one hundred percent. Suzanne moved back home to help him function as best he could and to take him to his therapy.

Jennie and Matt rallied to help Suzanne and her mother. Of course, her father was worried about Stein Injection Molding Co., and Suzanne knew its success needed a family member at the helm. To everyone's surprise, she enrolled in a part-time executive program at the Kellogg School of Management in Chicago, and she told her father that under his guidance she would assume management of the company. She would not let the company fail.

She commented to Jennie, "If I had listened to my father all those years, I would be an expert on injection molding, but now I have to learn the hard way. I never thought I would go from writing poetry to selling injection molding. Matt is so wonderful, I don't know what I would do without him. He has taken over the publication of my poetry so I don't have to worry about that, and now he is becoming interested in the process of making products and parts from plastic. It sounds simple, but it is a complex technology. His mind is always active."

"Suz, I'm so proud of you, helping your father and assuring him that the business won't fail, going to management school, you are awesome, always there for people. You helped me when I was in the doldrums. I can never forget all you have done."

"You know, Jen, I was a spoiled, ungrateful kid for a long time, but Dad didn't give up on me. I think its payback time. I just want to do all I can for him."

"What do your parents think of Matt?"

"Oh, they love him; they can't believe he is real. You should have seen the hippies I brought home from college! Mother wanted to call the exterminator when they left. My last boyfriend, Michael, had beautiful dreamy eyes with long straggly hair which he sometimes gathered into a ponytail. Dad couldn't bear to look him in the eye."

Jennie laughed and commented, "I remember a few of those," and she was interrupted by her phone ringing impatiently.

"Well hello, John," she said, turning to look at Suzanne who grimaced at the mention of his name. "I'm fine, and how are you?" "No, I'm busy, and besides I don't date married men. I found out a month ago when I was in Quincy."

John replied, "It's true, we have been at odds with each other for some time. I want a divorce, but she refuses to give me a divorce. After two years, we have nothing in common, so we go our separate ways."

Jennie said, "That's very sad. Incidentally, how is my book selling?"

"Its still selling though sales have slowed. It would help if you could autograph the books we have in stock."

"I'm going to Quincy this weekend to visit mother, so I'll stop in on Saturday and do that."

"That's great, see you then."

Jennie was anxious to get her car out on the road for a long drive. She turned on the radio which was set to the public station, and her favorite classical music filled the car. She likes this drive to

Quincy now. The familiarity of the countryside was comforting and beautiful in a quiet way with the placid beauty of undulating hills, farms, and the smell of sweet clover in the fields. Traffic was light now, and she stepped on the gas. Soon she was passing the usual franchise food restaurants and discount stores on the edge of town. The four-hour drive to Quincy is the furthest she has driven the car, and she liked the way it handled and hugged the road. Lynn and Roger were anxious to see it too; Roger felt smug about her taking his advice.

Jennie and her mother went to the bookstore, and upon seeing her, John smiled broadly and rushed to greet them. She signed several books, and then chatted with him for a moment.

"Have you started a second book?" he asked.

"Yes, I 'm writing my second book, and I bought a new car so I can get my independence back."

"Good for you, is the book a Harlequin romance novel?"

"No, its not the typical love story, with a prince, princess and a villain. It's about a girl named Betty whose dream was to marry a dashing man, have an elegant lifestyle and raise her children, but a tragedy took the life of the man of her dreams. That turning point in her life caused her to re-evaluate her dreams, and her life took on a whole new dimension. That's as much as I can tell you now."

"Is the story about someone we know, someone in this room?"

Jennie blushed and softly murmured, "It started out as my dream, but then I had to improvise and take the story in a different direction with a different character."

"I'd like to help you with the "they lived happily-ever-after ending," John said softly, then quickly changed the subject and asked, "What is the title?"

"The title is '**One Special Summer**.'"

"Sounds captivating, and like a best seller!"

While driving back to Chicago on Sunday, Jennie summed up the weekend's activities, and she thought of John. She liked him and hoped he and his wife would work out their problems and live a happy life together.

As soon as she arrived home, she called Suzanne. "Hi Suz, can we meet at Tony's?"

"Yes, let's, I'm bored, and I miss our lively chats. I'll see you there."

They wended their way through the crowded restaurant greeting familiar faces along the way until they reached the last available booth. Jennie was anxious for an update on Suzanne's father.

"Suz, how is your father doing?"

"He is doing so amazing. We couldn't ask for anything better from his recovery. His speech improves each day. He still can't hold a cup of coffee or button his shirt, but with continued physical therapy that will change. His yellow rubber exercise ball is always close by. He's real good about his therapy exercises."

Jennie told her about her visit and conversation with John at the book store, then wistfully said, "Even though he is married, I still like him."

Suzanne rolled her eyes and sighed, "Jen, forget him; don't muddy your life with problems you don't need."

"You're right, Suz. I know it's a situation to avoid; I wasn't really serious. Incidentally, when will your poetry be published?"

"Matt has finalized all the preliminaries, and we are waiting to hear from the publisher. Are you going to help me with book signs?"

"Yes, you can definitely count on me. Wouldn't miss if for the world. Now that we've had some practice, it'll be great fun. Does it have a title yet?"

"Yes, the title is 'Reflections of Cervantes" – do you think that sounds snobbish? I do credit Cervantes for my passion with poetry."

Jennie thought for a moment searching for the proper reply; she didn't want to disillusion her. "No, it isn't snobbish. After all, it will be directed toward the literary market. I think it will help to sell the book. "

"I'm glad you agree," Suz replied. "That's what I thought."

Like sisters they looked to each other for advice and inspiration in their writing projects.

"Incidentally, what do you think of your business classes at Kellogg?"

"The course is very interesting. I'm able to relate to everything through osmosis – from listening to my father, and if I wasn't totally in love with Matt, I would go for the instructor. His name is Tom Doyle, and he's a hunk, which probably explains why there are more gals than guys in his class. By the way, I learned that he lives in Lincoln Park."

"Like a lot of other people, and that reminds me that tomorrow is a work day. Thanks for your company – let's do this again soon."

When Jennie entered her apartment, she saw the blinking light on her telephone indicating she had messages. She picked up the receiver and dialed star ninety-eight to retrieve her messages. The recorded message began, "This is the emergency room at Quincy Hospital calling Jennie Rogers. Mrs. Ellen Rogers was admitted an hour ago, and your name was given as the person to contact in event of an emergency. Please call 216-957-4500 for further information on Mrs. Rogers."

Jennie gasped and, hardly able to control her shaking, she dialed the number and identified herself to the woman answering the phone. The woman asked Jennie for her relation to Mrs. Ellen Rogers, and Jennie replied that she was her daughter. She then told Jennie her mother was admitted with severe chest pains, but before she could be treated, she suffered a massive heart attack and died instantly. They are holding her body for disposition by her family. Jennie told her she was Mrs. Rogers' only child, she lived in Chicago, but she would be at the hospital tomorrow to take care of the necessary paperwork and make arrangements and then hung up. Momentarily, she was too stunned to cry, and the thought "I was just there" went over and over in her mind and finally tears welled in her eyes. She sat staring into space and crying, trying to put the woman's words into reality, thinking "I didn't say goodbye to her," and then thinking how can one say a final goodbye." She began to think logically and to make plans for tomorrow, what must be done and what would be done. She would call her boss to relay the news and get the week off from work. She glanced at her watch and even though it was late, she dialed Suzanne's number. Their friendship was what kept each other from coming undone, and Suz was the first person she needed to talk to. When Suz answered the phone, Jennie exclaimed, "She's gone — mother died."

"But Jennie, you were just there today, what happened?"

Jennie told her of the phone call and that she would be leaving early in the morning to drive to Quincy. Suzanne wanted to go with her, but Jennie knows she has a full plate of responsibilities with her father and her classes, so she told her she would stay in touch and let her know the funeral arrangements.

The day broke shimmering and moist after an evening shower, and it began to rain again as Jennie turned onto Highway 55 and picked up speed. The steady pit-pat of rain and the "swish-thunk," "swish-thunk" of the windshield wipers beating back the downpour were the only sounds. She kept both hands on the wheel and an even foot on the gas. She felt her knuckles tighten on the steering wheel as cars whizzed by, spraying the windshield with fresh rain. After several miles, the rain slowed to a drizzle, and soon the sun broke through the clouds with the promise of a warm, sunny afternoon. Jennie began planning the day's activities, the decisions that needed to be made without deliberation for there was no time. First she would go to Brody Funeral Home and make arrangements for them to pick up her mother's body at the hospital, go to the hospital, and then she would call her friend, Lynn. She will need her support to get through this week's ordeal.

The long, solitary drive provided Jennie an ideal occasion to collect her thoughts and make plans for her mother's burial. She will be cremated as her parents requested in their wills. Her mother's ashes will be buried next to her father's ashes in Quincy Cemetery. Her father's ashes were buried there because mother wanted a place to visit him. The grave marker is in place, and only mother's date of death will need to be added. Jennie thought, "It is so typical of mother to have all the arrangements made in advance to make things easier for me."

"I will have a memorial service in the chapel of the Presbyterian Church, and I will ask Rev. Rust to conduct the service. I know that would please mother. They had a close relationship since he was also from Boston, and they kept each other up-to-date on anything and everything that happened on the East Coast. Mother would want him to read the 23rd Psalm, and she had stated several times that Amazing Grace and How Great Thou Art were her favorite funeral hymns. Roger is in the choir and the main soloist, so I will ask him to sing those hymns."

Many thoughts continued to go through her mind as she was driving. Losing her mother was one of the saddest times in her life, and she searched for words to describe her mother. She lived an ordinary life overseeing my achievements however humble and rectifying my failings, and she was always there for father. She always seemed to be happiest doing things for others, serving on various committees, at the heart of every fund raiser, the one who got everyone to do what needed to be done. And, she always had the Band-Aid or the right words to heal hurt feelings. Jennie remembered her mother saying, "You have two hands: one for helping yourself and the other for helping others," and she lived her entire life with that premise in mind. In less than a year's time, I have lost the two people who meant more to me than anything in life. The love I felt for mother can never be replaced. The love I felt for Steve will always be remembered in my heart."

"When I think of everything, like mother being alone and the distance between us, it's good that death came suddenly, and she did not have a long lingering illness prior to death. She wouldn't have liked that, and it would have been difficult for me to help her. If it had to be, her passing was the perfect way to go. I'm so glad she was able to dial 911. When I think of the ways that I will miss her and it seems trivial to say this, but I know apple pie will never taste the same again. She was known for her delicious apple pie."

When she approached the city limits, she stopped for gas, and while the attendant was filling the tank and cleaning the windshield, she went inside and called Lynn. Lynn had just learned of her mother's death from a friend who worked at the hospital, and she said, "Jennie I want you to stay with us, and Roger and I will help you with everything that needs to be done. I don't want you to stay in your mother's empty home by yourself just yet."

Jennie replied, "Lynn you are the dearest and most thoughtful friend. I was sort of dreading staying where mother became ill and was abruptly taken by ambulance to the hospital. How can I ever thank you for all that you do for me?"

"I know you would do the same for me," Lynn replied, "But let's not elaborate on such unimportant matters now. What is your schedule? What can I do to help you?"

Jennie told her of her plan and said she will stop by after going to the funeral home and hospital.

"That's fine; I'll see you when you get here. We'll have lunch and talk," Lynn replied.

While having lunch, Jennie stated that the memorial service would be held Friday afternoon, and she outlined other preparations that she needed to accomplish today. She asked Lynn if she would go with her to talk to Rev. Rust since Lynn knows him well and Jennie simply knows him from her mother's conversations. Lynn wholeheartedly agreed to accompany her. She also needed to go to her mother's home to get her financial records and a copy of her will, and they will go together.

After their visit with Rev. Rust, Jennie drove down the beautiful tree-lined street that had been her secluded world until she went off to college. She noted several changes along the way, the Nelson's house was now green instead of blue, the Kessler's had put an addition on their home when the twins were born, and the street itself had been resurfaced. That reminded her of the kid's delight in riding their bicycles over the many bumps and dips they had to endure for so many years. She drove past well-tended gardens and mail boxes on cedar posts and then slowed down and inched toward the white, Cape Cod with the open front porch where she and Lynn spent many summers as they reigned over the neighborhood. Her mother's familiar bed of purple and yellow pansies welcomed her with their vibrant display of color.

As she unlocked the door and entered, she was surprised to see everything neatly arranged as if her mother had left to visit a friend and would be returning. The living room smelled of furniture polish and Endust, and her own room was as tidy and pleasant as always. She wouldn't hesitate to stay here alone. After finding the papers that she needed, she and Lynn returned to the car.

Jennie told Lynn that after tonight she would stay at her home because there was so much to do. Lynn offered to help and Jennie gratefully accepted her offer. She asked Lynn if she would like anything of her mother's, and Lynn expressed an interest in the hall chest with mirror in the entry as she has an eye for antiques, and she always admired its glossy mahogany finish. Jennie told her she would love for her to have it.

Friday finally came and clouds rolled in, but as the morning wore on, they casually drifted away and the sun shone through. The service was lovely and short. Jennie felt that Rev. Rust spoke for her as he intoned the following words: "We are gathered to celebrate a fulfilled life. Ellen Rogers lived her life with courage, joy and purpose. So, if tears come, they will be the tears of feeling the loss of a loving presence in our lives, but not tears of sadness for her death. She lived her life as if it was never-ending, and she sought God's guidance on all matters in her life. Thanks be to God for Ellen's life."

Roger's rendition of Amazing Grace was beautiful, and tears flowed down Jennie's cheeks as he sang her mother's favorite hymns.

The chapel was almost filled, and the receiving line long. Most people were strangers to her, but they told of their acquaintance and fondness for her mother. The Senior Center was well represented and they spoke lovingly of her mother. John and Diane Gardner came together; she was as attractive as he was good-looking, and Jennie hoped they would work out their problems and live a happy life together. Diane told her she had read her book and liked it very much.

After all the hugs and embraces that were hard to pull away from, her dear friends, Suzanne and Matt told her "if you ever need a helping hand, we are here for you." Jennie knows they are sincere; Suz has always been there for her.

During the weekends following the funeral, Jennie drove to Quincy to sort through her mother's possessions. A great deal of it will go to the church bazaar. On a Saturday morning, she sat on a stool in the kitchen surrounded by cardboard cartons feeling despondent and overwhelmed as she began to pack the contents of the aged, but serviceable cabinets. She had suggested updating the kitchen but her mother protested saying it was perfectly okay for her needs. Now someone else will make that decision.

Seeing the black plastic cat clock with eyes that blink brought a smile and laugh as she recalled giving it to her mother as a childhood Christmas present. She remembered going to Woolworth's with her father to select the present for her mother. "I can't believe mother kept that all these years." She stuffed it into a packing crate hoping it would bring a smile to someone else.

The dishes, glassware, and her mother's treasured Fiestaware pitcher were all too familiar. Crammed in the back of a cabinet was her Winnie the Pooh cereal bowl. She smiled and held it close thinking back to when she sat in her high chair each morning intently eating every bit of cereal to get to the bottom to see the picture of Winnie and the words, "All Gone." She put it aside with the rest of the items that held special memories – items she couldn't part with now. She grew up with everything in this house, and now she has to dispose of the contents of this sanctuary where her parents lived all their married years. Most of the items were rarely used yet her mother held on to them afraid to part with a once-cherished possession that had now become clutter. "I'll probably be just like her in my old age," Jennie mused.

When she came upon the Christmas plates, she thought of all the Christmases when her aunts, uncles and cousins would get together. Those were some of her fondest memories, and she put the plates aside. She would carry on the Christmas plate tradition.

In a closet she found her mother's old portable Singer sewing machine. "Mom treated it like a favorite relative, oiling and cleaning it regularly, so I'm sure it still sews beautifully. I remember mother making most of my clothes when I was in elementary school and how I was dressed differently than the other children. My clothes looked more like costumes – all frilly and lacy. When I entered Middle School, I rebelled and told her I wanted to dress like the other kids, so she never sewed for me again."

She kept her mother's jewelry box remembering when she'd asked Steve what she should give her mother for Christmas. He said, "Why don't you give her a jewelry box; she has jewelry scattered all over the house – a saucer with rings in the bathroom, a saucer with ear rings in the kitchen, and a tray of jewelry on her dresser. It's obvious she needs to be more organized." Jennie agreed. Now her mother had everything neatly arranged inside, and it was lovingly displayed on her dresser.

She rifled through a box of photos, old snapshots, her baby pictures, formal photographs of her mother and father, an accumulation of her lifetime. "I must sit down some day and put these together in albums," and she took the box with her to the car.

She sold some of the best furniture to interested acquaintances of her mother, held a yard sale, and kept treasured glasses, accessories and other cherished objects for her remembrance. She walked through the empty rooms, inspecting each one as if expecting an echo of voices or footsteps, but there was silence. Saying good-bye to the home that comforted and sheltered her all her life was difficult, but she was fortunate that the well-kept house sold quickly. Now her only connection to Quincy was Lynn and Roger Smith, and they vowed to be life-long friends.

Chapter Eleven

*D*uring the drive back to Chicago, Jennie thought about her friends and her lack of a social life. She has neglected her book as well. "I have a lot of catching up to do."

When she arrived home, Suzanne called, said she was glad she was home and that she had an interesting conversation with Tom Doyle, her professor at Kellogg. "I had some questions about an assignment, and we started talking about various things. You know how brazen I am! Anyway, he recently moved to Lincoln Park, and would you believe he lives in the duplex next to your brownstone. I told him about you, how we went to school together, our publishing success, and some other stuff, and he would like to meet you. Incidentally, he isn't married, but he may have been, I didn't ask about that—didn't want to be too nosy. I told him about Tony's being the favorite place to hang out in the area and suggested that we (you and me and Matt) meet there for dinner sometime. He said he would like that. He wants to get to know the area and meet some new people. Jen, you are going to love him. He is so good-looking."

"Wow, I wondered when you were going to catch your breath! He sounds very interesting. I have been lamenting my lack of a social life with men. Meeting him at Tony's is a good move – if I don't like him, I'm not in an awkward situation – I can just walk away, no excuses."

"Great, I'll call him back and tell him we will meet him at 8. I told him you would be returning from Quincy tonight."

"Suz, you sneak, you had this date all set up! I better get moving – want to make myself presentable. See you at Tony's at 8."

Jennie had never been thrilled with blind dates and would rather not be a part of them, but this one, this Tom Doyle, sounded different. After all, he was a professor at Northwestern's prestigious Kellogg Graduate School of Management, so he had to have something going for him, and Suz had made a point of telling her that he is good-looking. It will be interesting. She decided to take care with her makeup and choice of clothing. After careful study, she pulled on her cream-colored pants with the soft sweater of the same color and with a neckline that delicately plunged to show some cleavage, but not too revealing - just enough to tease. Smiling at her reflection, she liked what she saw, the clear brown eyes and heavy brows, the high cheekbones and smooth tanned skin. Her carefully highlighted brown hair shone with the glints of blonde that used to appear naturally whenever she spent summer days at the beach. She picked up her handbag and almost danced out the door.

When she walked into Tony's, Suzanne and Matt were at the waiter's stand reserving a table when a 6 ft., well-built man approached them with an easy smile and handshake. His brown hair was coarsely threaded with gray, and he was positively handsome in his navy cotton sweater, white button-down shirt, and perfectly pressed and creased jeans. Suzanne spotted Jennie and drew her close to them saying, "Jennie, I want you to meet Tom Doyle."

Tom looked pleasantly surprised as he heartily greeted Jennie. The waiter led them to a table, and Tom couldn't take his eyes off her. Jennie thought to herself, "He is a handsome college professor!"

The conversation was brisk as they were eager to get to know each other. Tom told them, "I am teaching economics, dollars and cents as we say, to bright and brilliant students at Kellogg, and in my spare time exploring Chicago."

He had recently moved here from Minneapolis. She wanted him to keep talking just so she could continue to watch his perfect face and his mesmerizing brown eyes. He apologized for talking so much saying "I guess you're just easy to talk to" and he smiled so sweetly she had to remind herself to breathe. She felt she had to know everything about this handsome man, and she wondered if he felt the same way about her. "Suzanne was right," she thought, "I am going to love him."

When they were leaving, Tom asked Jennie if he could call her, and Jennie replied, "Yes, I'd like that." It was mutual attraction at first sight.

As she was lying in bed, she wondered what his kisses would be like, and with that happy thought she fell asleep.

After the usual Monday morning production meeting, Jennie called Suzanne. "Suz, I'm in love. Thank you for introducing me to that wonderful man."

"I knew you would like him, and I could tell that he likes you. Did he get your phone number?"

"Yes, and I hope I hear from him soon. I'll keep you up-to-date."

Jennie didn't have to wait long to hear from Tom. Two days later she had just returned home from work when he called and asked if she would like to go for a walk. He said he normally ran or jogged when he gets home from work, and it was a beautiful evening for a walk. That surprised her as she also likes to walk or run for exercise; she and

Steve ran often. He told her he would walk over and meet her.

She hurriedly changed into white shorts, a navy tee, and her running shoes. The doorbell rang and Tom, looking incredibly handsome and muscular in a black T-shirt and white shorts, smiled at her as if he was genuinely pleased with her tall, shapely figure and long legs.

"I'm so glad you suggested going for a walk. During the past month while going to and from Quincy, I have neglected running and exercise." However, Jennie was naturally athletic, and she was in great shape. Her upper arms had no fat, just the gentle muscle of an active woman.

"Well, we'll do something about that; I'm almost a fanatic about exercise, and I like to run regularly. I'm happy that you do too. Let's do it often."

They decided to walk to the lakefront and jog on the bike path that runs along the beach.

After a brisk walk, they slowed their pace as they began conversing seriously. Tom slipped his arm around her shoulders and said that Suzanne had briefly mentioned her loss of someone close, and he asked her if she wanted to talk about it. Jennie told him about Steve, and Tom said, "We have a lot in common; Jane, my fiancée, and I were engaged and soon to be married when she was killed in a tragic car accident. Since then I have lived a quiet life by myself. It took me a long time to come to grips with it, so I know what you are going through

"Yes, I grieved for Steve and then decided that Steve would want me to get on with life and remember him, but not grieve. Since I have always wanted to be a successful writer, I decided to go back to school, and I enrolled in a creative writing class at Columbia. That's where I met Suzanne. She encouraged me to write about Steve and our lives together as a way of coping with his death. It turned into a memoir, and our instructor encouraged me to submit it for publication. That's how my first book came about. Suz and I have been close ever since."

"That's an interesting slant on how to cope with death. I presume it worked?"

"Oh, yes, it gave my life a whole new dimension. Eventually, I was able to accept Steve's death as an unfortunate fate, and it helped me to live peacefully with it. How have you dealt with Jane's death?"

"I guess you can say I tried to run from it. I was teaching at the University of Minnesota in St. Paul and decided I needed a change of scenery. The position at Kellogg was open, I applied and was accepted. So Chicago became my new home, but I brought my grief with me. It was then that I became absorbed in fitness and athletics; it was something I could do when my time and work permitted as I teach both evening and day classes. That along with time has been my means of escape. At first, I vowed to never marry thinking that no one could take Jane's place, but I've gotten past that."

All of a sudden they realized they had walked further than planned, and they quickened their pace on the way back. Tom saw that Jennie was a lively, vigorous, and fun-loving woman, and he wanted to spend more time with her.

That evening Jennie relived their walk and their conversations. She envisioned Tom as a high-energy, athletic, worldly professional, and she found him stimulating and exciting. They began spending more and more time together. There was something so warm and comfortable about being with him.

They talked about their parents and their families, and Jennie asked about his mother.

"She was an actress, a theater star. Her stage name was Beatrice Baker. She didn't make it to Broadway, but she played at many well-known theaters around the country. She did summer stock, the whole bit. Since she had to travel extensively, I became an only child. My father was a Psychology Professor so the two of us were grounded. He was my friend, and he was both father and mother. Mother wasn't cut out for the role of child rearing, but she was interested in me, and we had good times together. As I recall, she was always "on stage," even at home."

"I wish I would have known her – she sounds very interesting. Evidently, your father left a profound impression with you for you to follow his profession of teaching."

"It wasn't discussed, as I recall, but we were very close, and it just seemed the natural thing to do. At first I thought about joining the faculty of a small New England college near Boston. It was an attractive-looking campus with typical New England style brick buildings in a small town just three miles from the Atlantic coast. I then learned its major endowment was dwindling to nothing, and the school might go broke. I readily changed my mind and decided to stay in Minnesota."

Jennie looked forward to those evening walks when they hurried out into the fading sunlight like romantic lovers fleeing confinement or being liberated from their tedious obligations. On all the following nights that summer, they talked about almost everything they had ever done or hoped for. Of course, they laughed and kissed, too. His kindness, his good nature and sense of humor, his intelligence, and sweetness made it so easy to fall in love, and everyday she is conscious of being in love with him.

They discovered they liked many of the same things, and one of those mutual interests that surprised Jennie was Tom's love of cooking. Since he has been a bachelor all his life, of necessity he became quite adept at culinary skills, and this was reflected in his attractive, well-outfitted kitchen with its spacious countertops and colored appliances. The cabinets and drawers indicate he is a collector of gadgets.

Tom's apartment was a spacious duplex in an elegant limestone next door to her brownstone. However, inside it was a cool white contemporary home with contemporary furnishings and wall to wall bookcases filled with books and colorful contemporary paintings on the surrounding walls. They most often "hang out" at Tom's place dressed in faded jeans and bare feet. They love to experiment with new recipes and unusual seafood. They both preferred fish and chicken to red meat, unless it was a perfectly grilled steak.

When Suzanne graduated from her executive MBA program at Kellogg, Jennie and Tom invited Suz and Matt over for a lobster dinner which they raved about. Included was an appetizer of Brie en Croute with white wine, fresh asparagus with chopped egg and vinaigrette, and a creamy lemon cheesecake for dessert. Tom toasted Suzanne for graduating from his business course and for introducing him to an amazing woman.

Chapter Twelve

Having a man as a friend again was good for Jennie's ego. While taking care of her mother's property and belongings, her book was put on hold, but her romantic relationship with Tom renewed her interest and enthusiasm. Since her writing had dragged out, Matt had been prodding and cajoling her to finish her second novel.

Tom also encouraged her to write. He felt guilty taking up so much of her time, but they didn't want to be apart, so they decided to take their vacation together in a fishing cabin on one of the many fishing lakes in northern Minnesota. It was his favorite hideaway; a place he had gone often to fish and relax. As Tom pulled his car onto the gravely rutted road leading to the cabin and the lake, Jennie knew she was definitely entering a man's world, one she was not accustomed to.

The sea green cabin with dark red shutters sat like a refuge at water's edge, and it blended well with the heavily wooded forest behind it. The lingering smell of a fresh coat of paint greeted them as they entered. The great room in the cabin smelled of wood smoke that emanated from the huge fireplace made of river rocks. Off of the great room was the bedroom and bathroom. Sheets covered heavy pieces of furniture and light cotton curtains covered the paned windows. The dark wood walls were bare, and Jennie imagined the fish stories that were embedded in those walls, told by fishermen clustered around a roaring fire in rocking chairs on cool nights. The faded and worn linoleum floor was scarred from sand, heavy boots, and age, but there was a feeling of nostalgic good times in the room.

Yellow electric light poured from a hanging fixture that resembled an old kerosene lamp. The kitchen area consisted of an old chipped enamel gas stove, a farmhouse sink, and an ancient refrigerator on legs with a motor on top. The cabin was simple and spartan, but it was clean. Jennie was confident that the beauty and solitude of the lake would offer the inspiration she needed to complete her novel. They decided their mornings would be devoted to writing and fishing and in the afternoons they would swim and explore the area. Jennie had never been to northern Minnesota, and Tom was anxious to introduce her to a new world. The spring-fed lake was a joy to swim in, and the 2.5 mile walk around the lake was a refreshing hike. They both wore shorts and T-shirts and looked unnaturally pale, but after two weeks, their skin would be golden.

She set her Smith-Corona portable typewriter on a wooden table outside the cabin where she had a view of Tom fishing on the shimmering blue water.

The only sounds were the water lapping at the shore and the tap, tap, tap of the typewriter. While she wrote he would catch and cook their dinners. They watched the sunset over the lake as they dined on walleye and shared a bottle of Chardonnay. In the moonlight, they took long walks around the glistening water talking and laughing. As Jennie said, "We always talk too much as if we need to know everything about each other."

On one occasion they were discussing his job, and Jennie asked, "Have you ever had a student make a play for you?"

"Of course," he teased, "That's one of the hazards of the job."

"I'll ignore that conceited remark because I'm anxious to hear about her, or them, should I say?"

"Well, there was this student, she was a very attractive girl, who began some heavy flirting about two weeks before graduation – staying after class with questions, dropping in at my office to get a "lost" assignment, always lingering and moving closer, wanting me to get personal with her. A couple of times she asked if we could have dinner together. I told her not until she graduates. She said she couldn't wait that long."

"I knew she was testing me to find out if I would risk my job for an affair with a student. You see, in two weeks she would graduate and the laws pertaining to faculty fraternizing with students would no longer apply. I had an idea that after graduation she wouldn't know who I was. To find out if my assumption was accurate, about two weeks after graduation I called her, and a boy answered the phone. She told him she didn't want to take the call."

"Well, I didn't realize a professor's job could be so hazardous! Seriously, I can't imagine a student being so bold!"

After a morning of writing and fishing, Tom asked, "What shall it be?" "Long swim?" "Nap?" "Both?" Laughing, she said "both, of course." They dived off the dock for a long, leisurely swim and then went inside. She peeled off her wet bathing suit and slipped into a white terry beach wrap. Her wet hair was loosely braided and hung down her back. Tom pulled her close to him, and the beach wrap slipped off her shoulders, falling to the floor. He picked her up and carried her to the bed, and Jennie reached out and drew him close to her. Afterward they lay in each other's arms and napped until they were awakened by the grousing of blue jays outside their window.

"I could stay like this forever," Tom whispered.

"Me, too," Jennie said, snuggling closer.

"From the very first time I saw you, I've wanted you so much." He propped himself up and gazed at her. "You knew, didn't you?"

"Oh, yes," Jennie murmured, "I felt the same way."

"I think we have something very special, Jennie"

Before dinner, Jennie took a tray of frozen appetizer pastries from the freezer and put them in the oven. There was a mixture of crabmeat, minced mushroom and sausage pastries. When the timer on the oven range rang, in their ravenous state of hunger, they both rushed to take them from the oven, nearly forgetting potholders. Jennie playfully nudged Tom aside with her hip and removed them from the oven, then transferred them to a serving platter. Teasing, Tom said, "They smell delicious, you are a wonderful cook." He had opened a bottle of wine, and they took their glasses and pastries outside to enjoy the fading sunlight. A cool breeze was coming off the lake now offering relief from the muggy heat of the day.

One afternoon when they were stretched out in the red Adirondack chairs in front of the cabin, two deer in their beautiful russet summer coats emerged from the woods just yards from them. Jennie and Tom froze and remained silent as the deer suddenly became motionless, cautiously taking in their surroundings, their eyes like horse's eyes, shiny and black, alert to any danger, before proceeding to the lake where they quenched their thirst.

"What beautiful, proud animals, I'm surprised they came so near us," Jennie remarked.

Tom grasped her hand to silence her and directed his gaze back to the woods where a white-dotted fawn wobbled along on long shaky legs, stopping occasionally to munch on lichen. One of the does stomped her forefoot, and the fawn bounded to her side and to the water's edge to indulge in the clear blue water.

In reply to Jennie's remark, Tom said, "It's because we were still and silent — if they had seen movement, they never would have passed us. Deer are the most beautiful animals in the forest, and they are plentiful. I love the wild creatures and could never hunt them. But, unfortunately, hunters will occupy this cabin during hunting season, and the deer population will diminish."

"That's the first time I have been that close to a fawn. How old do you think it is?"

"Fawns are generally born in May and June, so it's about 2 months old. In the fall its spots will fade and by winter, its coat will be a gray-brown color. It's nature's camouflage to protect them."

After the two weeks at the lake, Jennie felt that **One Special Summer** was sufficiently complete for Matt's judgment. She dropped it off at his office and hoped he wouldn't make too many "blue pencil" corrections or remarks. However, because of the change of scenery and relaxation with Tom at the cabin, she felt confident and expected excellent remarks from Matt. "How strange that writing didn't seem a chore while at the cabin," she mused.

In the meantime, she wanted to get together with Suzanne to find out what she had missed while they were at the lake. They decided to meet at Tony's, and Suz told her she had good news for her. The first bit of good news concerned her father; he had improved tremendously, and Suz had taken him to the office in his wheelchair. Because he still had paralysis in his right leg, walking was difficult. He now had complete use of his right hand and was able to sign documents. The doctors say he might or might not have full use of his leg. He continues his therapy, so they are hopeful. Suz had become extremely engrossed in the injection molding business and wanted to take over full time. She was confident she could run the business. Her father would like to retire, and as soon as his leg improved, he and her mother planned to do some traveling. He was also thinking about buying property in Florida so they can spend the winters there.

"Jennie, you are looking at the future president of Stein Injection Molding Co."

"That is so wonderful; I'm really proud of you, Suz. Remember when you were a "spacey" student living in that noisy place called 'student housing?' I certainly didn't think you would ever end up being the president of a major company, did you?"

"No, I didn't – all I wanted to do was live the life of a hippie and write poetry. I wanted to experiment and follow the latest trends. When I met Matt, my ideas changed and I grew up. Hey, thanks for calling me "spacey.""

"Well, I really didn't mean that the way it sounded; you were just, let's say fun-loving. I think we both have changed, and I can't believe what has happened since then. Incidentally, how is your book selling?"

"Sales have slowed, but I'm not concerned. There's much more money to be made in the injection molding business. I could never make a living writing poetry, but it's a fun pastime, and Matt agrees. I disagree with W. H. Auden's remark in his "In Memory of Yeats" that "poetry makes nothing happen." I believe that a life without poetry is an impoverished life. It would be nice if more people read poetry and bought books of poetry so I could make a living writing them."

"There's been a lot of debate over that line, however, more importantly, how are things with you and Matt – will there be a wedding some day?"

"Yes, definitely – we have talked about it, just haven't set a date or made definite plans. What's the situation with you and Tom?"

"We want to be together forever, but haven't discussed marriage. Tom is older; he's forty-four, twelve years older than I am, and he acts like a confirmed bachelor, but I'm ready to get married. I can't imagine being with anyone else. Maybe he needs a little more time. Maybe he's afraid of having to go through a wedding; I would just as soon run off someplace and get married."

"Me, too, but I know Mom and Dad expect me to have a traditional Jewish wedding. You know, it's the "only daughter thing.""

"To change the subject, I dropped off my manuscript and I'm waiting to hear from Matt. I'm sure his comments will be favorable."

On Saturday afternoon, Tom and Jennie decided to spend the rest of the day at North Avenue Beach. Of course, they walked, carrying their towels, sun lotion, etc. Two young boys wanted to get a volley ball game going, so they joined them for awhile, and then stretched out in the warm sun to lazily chat. Tom asked about her book, and she told him she had made some changes and was waiting to hear from Matt. He knew how eager and excited she was at the prospect of having a second book published, and he said "I have a surprise for you when it is published." He didn't say if it was published, and his confidence was encouraging. Then they discussed their work and other generalities, and his mention of a 'surprise' was completely forgotten.

Fall was rapidly approaching, and Tom's teaching schedule would again become full time. He was already doing research for his dissertation and preparing class material. This year would be a busy one because he would also be writing a textbook to become a tenured professor. The job of a college professor is often glamorized, but in reality it was an extremely busy job with daily long hours. His days revolve around countless papers, theses, books, studies and grades, but he is doing what he likes.

He explained to Jennie, "A professor is not being paid $120,000 to shuffle papers. You must be creative, have ideas, and convincingly articulate them to your class. I try to teach them the "nuts and bolts" of economics and politics. I love to teach, and I care passionately about what we can do to make our economy fairer."

Jennie's stress was eased somewhat when she finally received a call from Matt. He abruptly told her they needed to discuss **One Special Summer**.

She had an uneasy feeling about the serious tone of his remark, and she hurried to his office. As she suspected, his comments were not what she wanted to hear. Barnett told Matt he thought the book was well written, he liked the people and what they had to say, but they never really did anything. It was as though Jennie invited the readers for dinner, but didn't serve any food. Jennie was deeply humiliated and went into a state of grief. She was frustrated and thought to herself, "I had good feelings about this book, especially the sections that were written while we were vacationing at the lake. I don't understand this failure; my first book sold well." She thought she was ready to become a successful writer; now she felt like a loser.

Matt continued, "Barnett's comment was that the story really wasn't about anything. It lacked a theme, it lacked cohesion. It didn't hang together, it was all over the place, and his final comment was that he felt reading it was a waste of time."

Jennie's head was spinning – a "waste of time!" She was scared and hurt, completely devastated. Her eyes glassed over, and her stomach was heaving. Too stunned to cry, she blurted out,

"Why didn't he just say it's total horse shit!"

Matt put his arm around her and tried to console her, "It has to be more than just a nice story; it has to make you think about it long after you've read it. Let's not start rewriting until we have a theme in mind and then we'll rewrite around that theme. Don't be so despondent. Don't kick your butt around the block – you can do it. I know you. You'll figure out what needs to be done and go at it. I'll be here to help you if you want help. Just don't give up."

Fear gripped her, and her voice quavered, "I don't think I'll ever be able to write again."

"All writers feel that way after a rejection, but to be successful, you just have to stick with it."

Jennie managed a weak smile and left.

To think clearly, she put the manuscript aside and licked her wounds for a couple of weeks. She discussed the book with Tom and Suzanne, who gave their suggestions and tips. Then she went to work going through the manuscript trying to salvage it. It was painful to eliminate some portions as she so liked the story that unfolded while she was with Tom alone for two weeks. As she rewrote the book, she told about Betty's first husband being killed in a tragic accident and then remarrying George before she had sufficient time to mourn her first love. At times she locked herself away from the world, and she was unable to communicate with anyone. George was a Korean war veteran who had his own problems adjusting to civilian life, and their lives were filled with turmoil because George had a tendency to exist comfortably without much thought beyond himself. He would tell you that he was one of the "forgotten ones" who fought in that Forgotten War. The demons in his head that he couldn't tell Betty about were driving a wedge between them, and they grew further and further apart. Added to that, he began drinking more, and they were spending less and less time together. He rationalized his drinking by saying the bar was less expensive than seeing a shrink. Finally, he realized alcohol was becoming a crutch, an excuse to remain dormant, and after much soul searching, he tossed his last glass of vodka off the deck, and he didn't have another drink since. Their lives changed dramatically as he became a counselor treating both alcohol and drug addicted veterans. He saw the need for counseling after he had successfully treated his own addiction, and he promised that no other veteran would be forgotten. During what Betty and George would later call their "one special summer," their relationship improved, finding its way closer to stable. With George's "clean head" and their revitalized feelings toward each other, they rediscovered their love and vowed to never part.

Weeks later Jennie delivered the revised manuscript to Matt and went home to await his verdict. She told him she would scrap the whole thing if Barnett didn't like the rewrite, but Matt encouraged her by saying "Almost all good writing begins with shitty first drafts. It happens to the most experienced writers."

Barnett's response was: "That was just what the book needed – some depth, compassion, and action." Now it will be published. When she told Tom that Barnett liked the rewrite and it would be published, he said, "Come over for dinner tonight, I have a surprise for you." Next she called Suzanne with the news and said, "This calls for a celebration with the four of us at Tony's on Saturday night."

When she entered Tom's apartment, they embraced, and Jennie asked, "What's the surprise, what have you been up to? Have you created the perfect crab cake?"

"No, funny face, hold out your right hand and close your eyes." Then he slipped a ring on her finger and asked "Will you marry me?"

Jennie hugged and kissed him and said, "yes, yes." He silenced her by taking her face in his hands exactly the way that every girl wants, and he kissed her with such softness that she could barely respond and had no choice but to stand there and let it happen.

As he held her in his arms, Tom told her his mind was made up the night that he met her, and he hoped she in time would have the same feeling. She admitted that she would have said yes if he had asked the question that night. They agreed it was mutual attraction at first sight, and they fell instantly and deeply in love.

While they were eating dinner, Jennie told him that Suzanne and Matt were going to help celebrate the sale of her book on Saturday night at Tony's, and asked if that would be okay. Tom said it would be perfect, now they have two things to celebrate.

They immediately began making wedding plans, and since neither of them has relatives in Chicago, they decided to have a small, private wedding ceremony over Christmas break, and fly to Mexico or the Caribbean for a honeymoon. They were anxious to begin their married life together.

Since it was October, time was a constraint. They not only had to consider Tom's busy end of semester schedule, but the availability of the chapel. First, they met with Reverend Paul Robinson at the First Presbyterian Church, and he agreed to conduct the service. The wedding would take place at 4 p.m. in the chapel on Thursday, December 19th, and they would be attended by Matt and Suzanne.

In addition to Matt and Suzanne, they wanted to include their closest friends as wedding guests. Jennie wanted Lynn and Roger Smith from Quincy to attend, and Tom would invite his fellow professor and close friends, Jim and Elaine Bowman. After the ceremony a photographer would take photos in the chapel prior to the dinner-reception at the Drake Hotel.

After looking at an array of travel brochures, they decided to fly to Cancun for a week. They were lured by its incredible white sandy beaches and incredibly blue water. They would go scuba diving, sail the tranquil sea for some sport fishing, soak up sun on the beach and spend romantic nights exploring its famous restaurants. The blissful honeymooners wanted to leave the snow and cold in Chicago and relax on the sandy beaches of Cancun.

The duplex that Tom owned would become their home. They had to decide which of their belongings they would keep and what they could part with to combine the two households. This they accomplished without arguments or hurt feelings. They respected each others wishes. Tom's king size bed would stay, but Jennie's elegant mahogany furniture would replace his contemporary furnishings. Jennie's traditional living room tables and lamps blended nicely with some of Tom's modern pieces. It turned out to be an eclectic mix of distinctive tastes.

At the start of the Christmas season, Jennie asked Suzanne to spend an evening with her shopping for her wedding dress. North Michigan Avenue was magical during the Christmas season, and its lights sparkled and twinkled like a fairyland. The fabulous light spectacle was the perfect background for shopping. Jennie fell in love with a winter white dress made of silk and wool that followed the lines of her body perfectly. She had the body of a swimmer, broad shoulders and slim hips. Her mother's diamond pin would be her only piece of jewelry aside from a faux diamond bracelet she treasured.

Tom and Jennie discussed writing their own vows as so many couples do nowadays, but decided they were two traditionalists who couldn't change their ways. And so Tom faced Jennie and clearly stated, "I, Tom, take you, Jennie, to be my wife, to have and to hold from this day forward, for better or for worse, for richer, for poorer, in sickness and in health, to love and to cherish; from this day forward until death do us part." Jennie repeated the same vow to Tom, and then the minister said, "Tom, you may now kiss the bride."

They then faced the small audience of close friends, and Rev. Robinson said, "I now present to you, Tom and Jennie Doyle." Jennie was radiant and looked terrific, and Tom smiled from ear to ear.

Lynn commented to Jennie, "You look like the happiest person alive." Jennie winked and replied, "That's because I'm married to a wonderful man.

Chapter Thirteen

When they returned from their honeymoon, Jennie devoted her spare time to promoting her second book, **One Special Summer**, which had just been released to the public. Matt scheduled book signings at various bookstores in the Chicagoland area, and Tom took time away from his own writing to help her. After reading her book, he commented that he could easily relate to the characters. Jennie replied, "Everything I write has to be connected to my life in some way, and I inject my personal feelings into the story – it's my way of making fictional characters become more like real people."

"Tom, I want to do another book sign in Quincy. I want everyone to be aware of my success as a writer; sort of a "local girl is celebrated author" success story. Would you please help me?"

"Of course, I'll do everything I can to help you, and, you have told me so many wonderful things about Quincy, I want to go there."

Jennie asked Matt to make arrangements for the "sign" at John Gardner's bookstore,

Waldenbooks, and she was anxious to hear John's reaction. Their marriage announcement appeared in the Quincy newspaper, so she expected she would be spared from having to surprise him with news of her marriage. She just wants an amicable, business relationship void of their previous personal relationship. Tom's presence will be helpful.

At daybreak on a Saturday morning, Tom and Jennie were on their way to Quincy. They decided the Grand Prix needed to be driven on the highway after hardly being driven since their marriage. Tom liked the way it controlled and he picked up speed and sped through the hilly countryside past the ever-present red barns and silver silos standing erect in snow-covered farmyards. The scenery is all so familiar to Jennie but Tom tried to absorb the beauty of this newly-discovered rural atmosphere. He liked the wide-open, uncluttered spaces that some people call boring. Then the smooth expanse of highway was interrupted by the ever-present potholes of winter, and he was startled out of his reverie.

As they drove up to the store, they were greeted by a large bunch of colorful balloons at the entrance, and Jennie felt this book sign would be as successful as her previous sign. It was still early, but she wanted to meet John and make certain her supplies had arrived. John was at the cash register, and he smiled broadly and rushed to greet them extending his hand to Tom. He said he was happy to see Jennie again and happy to meet Tom, stating that he saw their wedding announcement in the paper. Jennie immediately felt at ease and wanted to know what she could do to get ready for the sign.

"Well, you can autograph some books – I'm glad you came early."

Then he asked Tom to help set up displays They talked while working, and she half heard their conversation and laughter thinking how easily they make small talk and become acquainted, and how they are so much alike in that regard.

The store began to fill with people who were anxious to meet and greet Jennie telling her how they enjoyed her first book and now they want to read her second book. Without hesitation, they picked up a book and headed to the cash register. Tom looked at her with pride and admiration. John told him, "You are a lucky man!"

When John saw that Jennie had a free moment, he went to her and congratulated her on her marriage to Tom. He also told her that he and Diane had reconciled and were extremely happy once again. Then another wave of customers came in, and Jennie was busy chatting about the book and introducing Tom to acquaintances. A reporter from the local paper briefly interviewed her. Lynn and Roger were happy to see them again, and they wished her much success. Soon it was time to leave another successful book sign. John said he would send copies of any newspaper publicity to Matt. As they were walking to their car, Tom remarked, "I think it is safe to say that Quincy is proud of you – you are a celebrity!"

Jennie and Tom had discussed their desire to have a family, and at their ages they could hear their biological clocks ticking. After a few months of trying to get pregnant, she finally conceived, and they couldn't be happier. Their timing for starting a family couldn't have worked out better for Jennie. Her employer, Bradley Engineering, was in the throes of an economic downturn, and because she was one of the new staff members, her work would be integrated with other teams. As a result, she was given a nice severance package. Since she hadn't planned to continue working after the baby was born, this worked out well. Her second book was selling well; her life was becoming a dream come true.

At one time Jennie didn't think she would ever love a man with more affection than she had loved Steve. She will always think lovingly of Steve, but now Tom and their baby will fill her heart with the love that she has yearned for. She thought how her life seemed to have been enlarged suddenly – peopled, full of duties, chores and obligations - and pleasures. Exactly the things she longed for in life.

Her job no longer consumed her creativeness, and she had more time for writing; she would that is, until the baby arrives. Now that she has the financial security of marriage, she considered her life's ambition – a full-time writing career. "Am I truly prepared for the long haul, to stick it out through all of life's changes? If timing and conditions would ever be ideal, now is the time," she mused. Tom encouraged her to follow her aspirations, so she began to brainstorm her third book, which will be titled **Heaven Sent**, and she submitted an outline to Matt. The story would tell about Maria's, (the protagonist) surprise pregnancy and how it altered her life:

"Maria and Joe had married before he was shipped off to Vietnam. She became pregnant, and before the baby was born, Joe was killed in action. As he was dying, he asked his buddy, Tony, who was fighting alongside him to look after Maria and the baby. Later Tony's Jeep was hit by an enemy mortar round, and although he lost both legs, his first words upon regaining consciousness was "I want to go back to my unit." Then when he saw his shattered legs, he muttered "Damn, both of them?" After his discharge he recalled his buddy's request, and with scant information about Maria, Tony eventually found her. They immediately fell in love, but there was a family problem that would keep them from marrying. Maria was from an ancient Italian family who were bitter rivals of Tony's Sicilian family, and the parents objected to their marriage. But the lovers continued to see each other in clandestine meetings, and Maria became pregnant. Abortion was out of the question, so Tony must do the honorable thing and marry Maria. For the time being, the two families try to put their differences aside and await the arrival of their first grandchild."

When Jennie sat down to write each morning, her own morning sickness translated to Maria as she tried to fight her nausea. They both had much in common; the surprising and irrepressible body changes and the uncertainty of their future as mothers.

It was decided that Jennie should have the test which determines the sex of a baby, and the test indicated it was a boy. It didn't really matter to Jennie, but Tom was adamant in his desire for a son. He wanted to honor his father with a son, and he was steadfast in his desire to name the baby, Charles Thomas, after his father. His son will be known as "Charlie Doyle." They joked about that; will he be like good old Charlie Brown or like a character in a cowboy mystery as the name seemed to connote? Tom said, "He will take after his father and be Professor Charles Doyle – a third generation Doyle professor."

Suzanne's father was recovering well except that he probably will always have some paralysis in his right leg. He had progressed from a wheel chair to a walker or cane. Suzanne has taken over the business, and her parents are enjoying retirement.

Matt and Suzanne are anxious to get married, and they decided now is the perfect time.

Suzanne first broke the news to Jennie. "That is so wonderful – you and Matt are perfect for each other. When you're together, you're so totally together," Jennie replied. "I remember when you met – you went with me to his office to talk about the book – you were so funny."

"Yeah," Suzanne replied, "He had the cutest butt, but I think it was Bob Dylan who really sealed our fate."

Laughing, Jennie said, "I remember Dylan too – you were his biggest fan."

"I told Matt when I walked into his office an angel appeared and told me you were the man I would marry. He just smiled, recalling the Jewish legend. I'll tell you about that some day."

"I want you to be a part of my wedding. Our witnesses have to be Jewish, but I would like you to be my honorary Maid of Honor. You won't have to do anything, just accompany me to the chuppah and be at my side."

"I would love to be your honorary Maid of Honor; it would mean so much to me. You have been a wonderful friend. I hope the wedding will be soon so I'm not huge and waddling down the aisle."

"Don't worry – you are the prettiest pregnant woman I know. The date is Tuesday, June 7th. We will have a small ceremony at Temple Sholom, mainly family, and a reception at the Drake. Both Matt and I come from small families. Mom and Dad have been dropping subtle hints, like grandchildren, but Matt and I are anxious to be married soon – we've been engaged for about a year now."

"Jen, will you help me shop for a dress? I'll sneak away from the office some afternoon - I'll let you know when."

"Yes, I would like to. I'm free almost any time. I'll wait for your call."

Suzanne decided to first go to Field's to look for a dress, but nothing stood out or spoke to her one way or another, so they proceeded to go to Neiman-Marcus. There she found the perfect dress, the one that she had seen in her mind over and over. It was a long white strapless silk gown with a fitted beaded bodice of pearls and rhinestones, and the skirt which was slightly flared at the hemline fell gracefully to the floor. It fit Suzanne as if it was made to her measurements. Suzanne is tall and slender, and the dress was exquisite in every detail. A pair of white satin sandals was the perfect accompaniment.

"Suz, you look gorgeous, a beautiful, happy bride."

145

Tom was spending more and more time at his office working on his second book. The first, which had gotten some attention in his field, had been an expansion of his doctoral thesis. But this book is more ambitious, more consuming. The book, entitled, "The Economic Growth of China," examines the economic reform in China since 1970 to illustrate the extent to which recent reforms were used to bring China to the forefront of the world's economic stage. He wanted to finish it by the end of summer because it would be important in his getting tenure. He had been working on it every minute he could spare from keeping up with his course.

Jennie also tried to devote time each day to her book. Initially, she wrote in the morning, but since her nausea was worse in the morning, she has been writing in the afternoon. Occasionally, Matt called to make sure she hadn't forsaken her book. Because her first two books sold well, he was anxious to represent her third book. She knew that her writing time may be limited after the baby was born so she must take advantage of these last few months without the distraction of regular feedings and diaper changes.

She also busied herself getting the baby's room ready and shopping for clothes and other necessities. One day she was able to talk Tom into putting his book aside and helping her shop for a crib, stroller and car seat. She didn't expect him to take much interest, but he became almost obsessive spending an inordinate amount of time comparing the pros and cons of each item. He was determined that their son would have only the best and safest product that is available. She was beginning to tire and was willing to settle for what looked the best to her. But not Tom; he is very energetic, and when he is enthused or excited, he is in constant motion. She has visited his classes, and he is always in motion there too.

She sat down and reached into her bag for a cracker. Her feelings of nausea occured more frequently now so she has been carrying a baggie of unsalted crackers in her purse. She took small nibbles of the cracker with swigs of water from the bottle she also took with her wherever she went.

Tom asked, "Honey, are you okay?"

"It's just the feelings of nausea that occasionally creep up on me. I'll be okay. You take your time."

"I think we're finished," and he took her arm as he guided the shopping cart with the other arm. "If there isn't a long line at the checkout counter, we'll be out of here in no time."

The crib and the stroller were delivered the following week, and Tom's mechanical adeptness was put to the test when the stroller arrived unassembled in a box. Tom remarked "I guess I have to get used to this. We may spend many a Christmas eve putting toys together." They opened the box and spread everything out on the living room floor and amid laughter and a few "oh, shits," the stroller was assembled.

Jennie put the bed linens on the crib, the mattress cover, sheet and coverlet, and put the baby's garments in the small dresser she had emptied for his clothing. Out of necessity, the spare bedroom would function as the nursery. The double bed was moved against the wall to make room for her mother's rocking chair, the changing table and the crib. She would sit in the rocker when nursing, and if the baby was ill or having trouble getting to sleep, she could stretch out on the bed to be near him or put him in the bed with her and not disturb Tom's sleep. This room arrangement would work well. They had talked about buying a home, but they both love living in close proximity to Lake Michigan in Lincoln Park and decided to wait until the baby approached school age. "Besides, we aren't 'suburb' people. We thrive on city life. The thought of mowing the lawn every Saturday doesn't appeal to Tom, and flower beds and carpools don't appeal to me."

It surprised Jennie that she was outgrowing her clothing so quickly, in particular her pants. After two months her waist began to thicken and then it disappeared. A friend suggested a maternity shop that carried the trendiest outfits, and it became her favorite store. Mothers-to-be no longer disguise their protruding stomachs, and she went along with the trend. She likes the smocked blouses and the pants with the "secret belly fit" stretchy insert.

She had hoped she would be able to wear her favorite summer evening dress for Suzanne's wedding, but she was just too big. At what has become her favorite shop on Michigan Avenue, she found a pale teal dress with spaghetti straps and smocked waist. It was perfect for dressy summer evenings. She bought a pair of silver sandals with three inch heels, and she would carry a trendy silver handbag to complete the outfit. Her faux diamond bracelet would add some glitter.

Chapter Fourteen

Tuesday, June 7th, dawned gray and oppressive, but early in the afternoon east winds off Lake Michigan shifted (as often happens), and the lakefront breezes drove the clouds and heat away from the city. It was as though someone turned on the air conditioning; it is not an unusual weather event in Chicago.

Jennie was especially pleased; she wanted her friend's wedding to be beautiful and perfect in every way. She and Tom arrived early to prepare for her role in the ceremony. The Rabbi summarized the various steps of the wedding ceremony.

Suzanne was radiant in her wedding gown. She had pearls twined in her upswept red hair, and her bare shoulders gleamed against the silk of her dress. She was beautiful, elegant and slender. Her mother, with her newly-curled strawberry blond hair, literally glowed in an Oleg Cassini blue sequin dress with matching glittery blue eye shadow on her eyelids, and her father looked puffed up and proud in his crisp black tuxedo. It was evident that this was an event they had been looking forward to for a long time.

The best man and maid of honor then escorted Suzanne and Matt to the chuppah or wedding canopy. Their parents and Jennie, as an honored guest, walked down the aisle and took their place under the chuppah.

At the close of the ceremony, a glass of wine was poured, and the seven blessings were sung, after which Suzanne and Matt drank the wine. Then the Rabbi wrapped the wineglass in a linen napkin, and Matt crushed it under his heel. The guests rejoiced saying Mazel Tov!

When Jennie and Tom arrived at the reception they were greeted by Suzanne and Matt and their parents. Jennie and Suzanne embraced, and Jennie wished her well. Matt's parents had flown in from New York, and they were greeted warmly. It was evident that Matt's tall stature and good looks came from his father.

Dinner was preceded by the traditional toasts. Suzanne's mother rose and stated, "Suzanne, my darling daughter, your father and I are so very proud of you today. You were – you are – the most wonderful daughter anyone could ever ask for, even if you drive me crazy sometimes…Suzanne smiled, and she did too. You're the best thing I could have ever hoped for. I know that you and Matt are going to have a wonderful life together."

After dinner an orchestra played and everyone drifted to the dance floor. Tom stood and led Jennie to the floor. It had been sometime since they danced together, but all she had to do was let the closeness of his body tell her what to do. He was a wonderful dancer. Between dances they stood close to each other, waiting for the music to start again, for their bodies to be close again. They were a handsome couple, and their happiness drew admiring glances from everyone on the floor.

Suzanne and Matt were taking a honeymoon trip to San Francisco, and when they returned Suzanne would move from her parent's home in Lake Forest to Matt's high-rise condo near the lake in Lincoln Park. The four friends would continue to be near each other in Lincoln Park.

Jennie was now in her sixth month of pregnancy, and she had outgrown morning sickness and was feeling good. Tom's book was nearing completion, and they had more time to spend together. They took long walks around the lake savoring the last days of summer. At Suzanne's wedding she barely looked pregnant, but now her breasts and her belly were swelling more. She had thought that Tom might think her figure was repulsive, but he told her she looked more beautiful than ever, and he liked to pat and rub her protruding belly. She and Tom were extremely happy. All she wanted was an occasional hot fudge sundae – that was her only food craving thus far during her pregnancy. They often stopped at the ice cream shop after walking, and Tom made certain there was ice cream in the freezer. He said, "I don't want to be dispatched at all hours of the night going in search of a hot fudge sundae."

September arrived and children with freshly-scrubbed faces dressed in their new back-to-school clothes lined up at corners waiting for the school bus. When seeing the children, Tom pondered his new role as a father. He began to mentally prepare for the baby's arrival the end of November. He would make certain that Charlie had everything he needed to grow up active and healthy. His mother can teach him how to dress himself and when to say please and thank you, and he will teach him all the things that boys need to know like baseball, football and basketball. They would go to the lake, and he would show him how to bait his hook and teach him how to fish. He hoped that Charlie will want to do all the things he likes to do.

Tom's classes also resumed, and it would be another busy academic year. He had posted his available office hour schedule on his office door, and it was filling rapidly with students desiring academic advice and career counseling. He also would meet with prospective students and attend committee meetings. All this in addition to delivering three lectures a day, printing handouts, grading papers, and replying to as many as 20 messages a day. During his lectures, he tried to connect with each student by asking questions, making eye-contact and encouraging them to participate. He liked to have a lively exchange of ideas, and he was animated as he moved from one end of the room to the other. If a student was sleeping he would be embarrassed when he is called on to participate.

Tom loved teaching – he loved the interplay of the students' minds with his own, and he loves their unpredictability, and occasional outrageous questions. His work day started around 6:15 a.m. at his home office when he read and replied to his mail, and it ended in his home office in the evening grading papers and preparing for the next day's lectures. Tom wonders how he will find time to be a good father.

Jennie had a constant reminder that her new role in life would be preoccupied with a baby boy named Charlie. She was getting bigger and bigger and could no longer hide her belly in anything other than a tent. To take her mind off the obvious and, of necessity, she spent more and more time at her typewriter creating and writing knowing that time would be a precious commodity after the baby arrived. She began to plan her schedule around feedings and naps knowing that Tom's daily involvement would be extremely limited, and activities as a family would be relegated to weekends. She was well aware of the many obligations and demands of a college professor, but she knew Tom thrives on those obligations and demands and wouldn't want to do anything different. He told her he didn't want to become a college professor for the money, although the salary was comfortable, he wanted to teach – to enlighten the minds of students.

The phone interrupted her thoughts, and she was happy to hear Suzanne's voice asking "Are you free for lunch?"

"Yes, Suz, what do you have in mind?"

"I don't have to be back at the office until after lunch so can we grab a bite together?"

"I would love that."

"I'll drive by and pick you up in 10 minutes – okay?"

"Great, I'll be outside waiting."

Jennie had just stepped outside when Suzanne's Buick swung next to the curb. As she settled herself in the front seat, she asked, "What is the reason for this mysterious hurried lunch date?"

"Well, I'm pressed for time, so I'll tell you all about it over lunch. There's a sandwich shop in the next block – let's have a cup of soup and a sandwich - is that okay?"

"Yes, I'm anxious to hear your story."

After the waitress took their order, Suzanne said, "I just came from the doctor's office, and I'm pregnant. Can you believe it! It must have happened on our honeymoon."

"That's wonderful news, Suz. I'm so happy for you. Does Matt know?"

"Not yet – I'll tell him tonight – I didn't want to just blurt it out on the phone. I can hardly wait to see his reaction. I just know he's going to be the proudest guy in the world."

"He will be a wonderful father, how far along are you?"

"The doctor said about two months. Oh God, I hope I don't have to go through morning sickness."

"Its not that bad really – just carry some unsalted crackers and water with you. It only lasts for a few months and after that you'll feel great. I can tell you just what to expect in your pregnancy and how to get through it. Are you going to be tested for the sex of the fetus?"

"Yes, I think I will – I would like a girl, but I'm sure Matt will want a boy. If we find out in advance, we won't have a big disappointment on what should be one of the happiest days of our marriage."

"Your parents will be ecstatic," Jennie replied.

"Yes, they will be delighted – they have been talking about grandchildren for ages – I think they were afraid I wouldn't marry and they wouldn't ever have grandchildren. I'll call them tonight."

Tom was surprised and pleased when Jennie told him the news. "Now Charlie will have a pal to play with," he said. "Don't be so sure," Jennie replied, "Suz wants a girl."

Chapter Fifteen

Soon after learning of her pregnancy, Suzanne lamented her tight-fitting clothes. She called Jennie saying, "My pants are too tight in the waist – I can't button them."

"I had that same problem at two months – my waistline just disappeared."

"Mom and I are going shopping for "fat clothes, would you like to go along?"

They went to the same maternity store where Jennie bought pants with the "secret belly fit" which they thought was humorous, but terribly ingenious. While at the store, Suzanne's mother looked at baby books and bought one for Suzanne and Matt.

"Oh, a "firsts" book," Suzanne exclaimed. "Mom, do you still have mine?"

"Yes, I do, Suz – I'll try and find it for you."

Suzanne went on, explaining to Jennie – "its more like a scrap book, and it starts with my ID bracelet from the hospital, my first photo, my first dress and little shoe, a lock of hair from my first haircut, a tattered piece of pink satin binding from the blanket that never left my sight, my first tooth, and the braces I wore later. I could go on and on – mother saved all my "firsts," and it's so much fun to look at it now."

"That's a wonderful idea; I'm going to do the same for Charlie."

"It's so cute that you actually have a name for your baby – I feel that I already know Charlie. After I have the ultrasound test, Matt and I will pick out a name for our baby."

Jennie's doctor visits were so regular now she could spread her legs in a stirrup without being embarrassed. During an examination, Dr. Kantor asked, "Have you thought of taking a Lamaze class or do you know about Lamaze?"

Jennie replied, "I've hear of them, but haven't looked into them."

"Well, your hospital, Children's Memorial, offers classes, and I would suggest that you consider a class now that you are in your eighth month. The class will prepare you for labor and birth, and it's a good idea to learn the signs of labor and the progress you will take from labor to birth. The class will help to eliminate your fears, and they will inform you as what to expect for a normal birth and how complications are handled. If you know what to expect you will be more relaxed, and you will have a more pleasant delivery. I'm not saying there isn't pain, that you must expect, but they will also cover the various procedures to lessen the pain such as an epidural. Of course, Lamaze stresses natural childbirth, but they also educate women that when interventions are needed, they are able to give informed consent. The classes also advise how your husband can be of help to you during labor and when it's time for you to call your doctor. We like to have husband's attend the classes, too. I can sign you up for a class, if you like."

"Yes," Jennie replied, "please sign me up – they sound so helpful, and I don't want to go to the hospital scared to death. But my husband won't be able to attend – he's a college professor, and he has a very busy schedule every day."

Dr. Kantor nodded and replied, "You will definitely benefit from their classes. I'll have my assistant get you enrolled as soon as possible, and she will call you with that information. I want you to be relaxed and confident that childbirth is a very pleasant experience."

Jennie couldn't wait to tell Suzanne about this new event in her life, and reiterated everything to her.

"I wish we could take the classes together."

"Me, too, Dr. Kantor said its best to take the classes in your seventh or eighth month so that everything is fresh in your mind when you go to deliver. He said its best if husbands and wives take them together, but Tom just can't get away. I hope that Matt will be able to go with you – its less scary if both of you take the class."

"Yes, I can relate to that. Matt is such a softy, he would probably pass out at the sight of the baby being delivered. But I think Tom could handle it – from seeing him perform in a classroom, nothing would rattle him."

Jennie laughed, "I agree with your assessment of Tom – he would probably pitch in and help the doctor or want to take over completely."

Her eighth month flew by and so did the fall color. Jennie missed her long walks with Tom along the lake with brilliant red, gold and orange leaves crunching underfoot. They both looked forward to their walk after dinner when Tom recounted the day's activities and his personal relationships with his students. He was concerned that none of his students fall behind; he considered it a reflection of his teaching ability. His students were almost like his children, and they treated him with respect and gratitude. She knew he would be a good father to Charlie.

One day when she woke, she felt her first contraction of labor, and a gush of water left her.

She became frightened; she wasn't ready for this. She hadn't finished her birthing classes; she had two more to go, and she hadn't packed her bag yet. But, thank God, it was Saturday.

She brushed her teeth, washed her face, and brushed her hair. She went to the kitchen to make coffee, and she had another contraction. She looked at the clock; the interval had been 12 minutes. Tom entered the kitchen, poured a cup of coffee, and Jennie told him what had happened. She had another contraction, and this one was ten minutes later. She called Dr. Kantor, and got his answering service. She told the woman on the phone what happened, and she was told to go to the hospital.

Tom and the nurse were urging her like cheerleaders to push, push, push. Beads of perspiration on her forehead glistened under the lights as she gave a final push, and suddenly the baby was out of her. The nurse grasped the red slippery, wailing baby and left. Dr. Kantor enthusiastically said, "It's a boy," but all she wanted to do was sleep. Tom kissed her, saying "I love you, sweetie."

Soon she was propped up in bed with Tom sitting at her bedside, and a nurse brought in a little baby wrapped in a blue blanket and laid him in her arms. Tom hurried to take a look at him and said, "he looks like a Charlie!" He had lots of brown hair and his face was slightly pink but clear. Suddenly a frown crossed his face and he stiffened a bit, then he opened his eyes wide and looked around. If he was able to discern his surroundings, he saw a proud father grinning at him and calling him Charlie.

Dr. Kantor entered the room and asked Jennie how she was doing. Jennie replied, "I am fine; how is Charlie?"

"He is very healthy, and his lungs are clear and strong as you will soon find out." He told her he was happy that she was going to nurse him and told her the nurse would help her get started. He told her she needn't worry about a feeding schedule; the baby will let her know when he was hungry and when he wanted to be changed.

Jennie asked him about going home, and he said, "There aren't any complications, everything is normal, so you can go home tomorrow or Monday."

Jennie said, "I would like to go home tomorrow; Tom has to work on Monday."

Suzanne and Matt could hardly wait to see Charlie so they stopped by for a short peek on Sunday evening. "He is the most beautiful baby boy!" they exclaimed.

"Charlie definitely takes after his father – he is so energetic," Jennie was telling her friend, Lynn Smith in Quincy, "and I can't believe how he is growing. At two months, he has already outgrown some of his baby clothes."

"I can hardly wait to see him in person – thanks for sending pictures of him. When the weather gets warmer, we'll drive up to Chicago to see him," Lynn replied.

"We would love to see you and Roger any time," Jennie said as she ended the call.

It was a cold day in January, and the winds coming off the lake were brutal. Jennie decided to stay indoors and catch up on social obligations. There were calls to make and thank you notes to write. They had had a busy Christmas with holiday parties, and their evergreen-bedecked home welcomed friends for an open house gathering. It was their first Christmas party, and she followed family tradition and used her mother's Christmas plates. Another family tradition was the spiral-cut ham and other cold cuts, huge salads, and dozens of freshly-baked rolls that brought compliments from everyone.

The big event of the season was Northwestern University's Christmas bash for the Kellogg Business School faculty and their wives. It began with cocktails, then a sumptuous buffet, followed by dancing to Les Paul's orchestra. Jennie had lost her pregnancy pounds and was able to wear a gorgeous black designer dress she had bought on sale for just such an occasion.

Jennie asked her friend, Denise, who lived in her old apartment building next door to baby sit that night. It was Denise who was with her the night she went to Tony's for pizza and saw Steve there with another woman, and they have remained good friends. It was the first time they left Charlie with a sitter, and he slept peacefully until they arrived home. Then he was wide awake and wanted to play, and Jennie wanted to sleep. She rocked him in the rocker while feeding him, and soon he was sound asleep.

Charlie is able to look around at his surroundings now and focus on objects. The Christmas tree seemed to mesmerize him, and he would gaze at it for a long time. They took a picture of him in front of the tree for his book of "firsts." On Tuesday, January 14th, he will be two months old, and his birthday cake will be a cupcake with a candle in the center.

Charlie looks like Tom, but he was mommy's boy. In the morning when he sees Jennie his eyes lit up, he smiled broadly, and he waved his arms around like he is really happy to see her. Who wouldn't melt with a greeting like that! Suzanne quickly put those thoughts into poetry:

He has his father's eyes and nose,
But his mother's smile and voice he quickly knows.
He's growing up fast,
going on twelve months old,
And so strong,
he'll quickly have you in a wrestling hold.
To his parents he is king of all,
Even though he is barely 2 feet tall.

At Matt's encouragement, Jennie was spending more time on her novel now. He confided that his business was slow, and he was reduced to reading and rereading the slush pile hoping to find a novel that would excite him and make it to the best seller's list.

"As an agent, I considered myself insulated from the downturn of the economy. I thought recession was something that affected factory workers, not the academia field. I hear the same from editors and publishers – they just aren't getting enough good material. Most of what they receive needs to be edited and revised before they could even consider publishing it, and those are few and far between."

Jennie told him now that her pregnancy is behind her, she is more enthusiastic and her mind is clearer so she is writing more and better.

"Matt, I would like to finish it sometime this spring before we go into summer when I know I'll want to be outside with Tom and Charlie."

"That's great, Jen, it's good to have a goal to work toward. I'm looking forward to your third book; I'm sure it will sell."

"We writers are a strange breed – we sit down and work on something that doesn't exist and we do it for weeks and months and years with the idea that someone might publish it and others might read it. People think you're an expert when you write a book; they don't know what we go through."

"Doubt and uncertainty are a part of the writing process for everyone, not just you. But we get used to it," Matt replied.

Large flakes of snow were falling, and while Jennie worked on her book, Tom was grading and correcting student's test papers. His comments were detailed and critical, but encouraging. "I can almost see their future, the type of person they are going to become in life," he told Jennie. "I can see their ambition, discontent or talent in their comments. They don't realize their life becomes an open book before me."

After Tom finished grading papers, he made a fire in the fireplace. Jennie curled up on the rug in front of the fire, and Tom joined her. Outside the wind gusted, but inside the fire burned blue and gave off steady heat. They wrapped themselves in the sofa throw, sipped a glass of wine, and talked and laughed and kissed. They had easily eased back into their normal sex life after pregnancy. Tom drew her closer to him before the dying logs, and then they were quiet. They snuffed out the last ember and went to bed.

On a bitter cold day in January, Jennie surprised Matt with the completed **Heaven Sent** manuscript. He was overjoyed and looked forward to reading it. Jennie was anxious to hear Barnett's comments.

Three weeks later Matt called and from the sound of his voice, she knew his response was not going to be what she wanted to hear. He told her Barnett liked her book except for the last several chapters; he thought the plot felt unresolved and flat, and it would be too much of a disappointment to the reader. Jennie disagreed, and she was adamant in her refusal to make changes. She wanted Matt to submit the book to a different publisher. Matt advised against that, and he was firm with Jennie, telling her "If Barnett says there is a problem with the plot, you have to address it. You can't ignore it. You can find your own solution, but you have to do something. When he makes suggestions for changes in a manuscript, he doesn't expect to be ignored. He isn't wrong, he knows what sells, and when there's a problem, we need to work on it.

Come into the office, and we'll go over it." Matt continued, cautioning Jennie to think of her future, "Jennie, he said, "you could have a loyal relationship with the most distinguished publishing house in the country."

Jennie quickly recalled Professor Baird telling the class they should heed the advice of their agent; they are more knowledgeable than you might think, and they know what sells and what doesn't. She thought for a moment, and then acquiesced; she didn't want to lose her agent or her publisher.

"Matt, because my second and third books have been rejected, I'm beginning to feel that I was a flash in the pan or just plain lucky with my first book. Can I really have a writing career?"

"You're being too hard on yourself, Jen. With **A Brief Wondrous Life,** you were passionate, and you wrote from the heart because of the love you and Steve shared. It would be very difficult to duplicate those feelings."

Sitting at her desk with the rejected manuscript staring her in the face, she felt her mind congeal and go blank. But she stayed with it and as she read and reread the sections that Barnett disliked, she realized she had been too protective of the main characters. They were too passive, and their lives were too serene. The story needed some conflict, and then the readers needed to be kept in suspense for awhile until the conflict was resolved.

In her rewrite she pointed out that even though Maria and Tony's parents had lived in America since the twenty's, they still lived in their country's old ways. But for the younger generation like Maria and Tony, it was the war that determined their lives. Vietnam, later shortened to "Nam" because it was mentioned so often, not only tore their lives apart, but the country as a whole, so their parent's in-family fighting was the ultimate in pettiness. Evidently, the stress that the parents added to their lives, in addition to Tony's difficulty as a double amputee in finding employment, caused Maria to go into premature labor which was life threatening to the baby. As a result, her doctor put her on complete bed rest until she finally delivered a perfectly healthy baby girl by cesarean. Maria's condition caused the parents to put aside their ethnic differences and in-fighting, and Tony finally succeeded in landing the plant manager's job that he so desperately wanted. In the end the two families were united, and Maria and Tony lived happily ever after." Her revisions strengthened the plot, and made it more interesting.

Weeks later, Matt called with good news: Barnett approved her revision. In fact, he gave the book glowing reviews, stating, "Jennie Rogers has become one of the most acclaimed authors of her time." Jennie was supremely happy. Now she could have three novels on the best seller's list.

Tom was duly impressed and asked, "What are you going to do for an encore – do you have something in mind?"

"Yes," Jennie replied, "I have an idea that I'm mulling over in my mind. Rachel Clark is a young star in the publishing business and is within reach of landing her dream job as a senior editor. She is about to marry her dream guy, and she has just purchased her dream apartment in Manhattan where the young and successful professionals hang out. She was assigned the job of editing a book written by the superstar of the literary world, the handsome and brilliant, Brian Howard. She loses her professional cool, falls for him, breaks off her engagement with her dream guy, then Brian Howard goes off to live in Tahiti. The title will be "**The Man of her Dreams**."

"Wow, you're being a little rough on Rachel, aren't you?"

"Not really, there's a lesson to be learned, and you have to be honest with your readers to retain their attention."

"I'm sure it will do that and be well written. I'm really proud of you, Jennie."

She ran this synopsis by Matt, and he said "go for it, make it entertaining and hilarious." And so, Jennie would begin her fourth book, a satirical comedy of literary life.

Tom was nearing the end of another school year, and they were considering going back to northern Minnesota for their vacation. Jennie had had happy dreams of those two weeks when they walked, swam, and fished together. She remembered the lazy afternoons when they napped and made love in the warm cabin as cool breezes from the lake blew the gauzy curtains back and forth and cooled their bodies. They fell asleep to the sound of waves slapping against the dock pilings. They would always remember those two weeks, they didn't have to consciously plan things, they evolved by themselves. But, this vacation will be different. They are parents of a little boy who will demand their time and attention.

Over a month ago Suzanne stopped going to the office everyday. Her lower abdomen was large and firmly rounded, and it was extremely uncomfortable to sit in one position for any length of time, and she wanted time to prepare for the baby's arrival. Her parents were so eager to have a grandchild, they want to spoil her before she even entered this world. Suzanne's mother insisted on taking her shopping for a crib, high chair, and stroller, and she constantly bought cute little outfits. Plus, she has had two showers so there wasn't much more that she would need. All the baby needs now was a name. Suzanne liked the name, Lauren; Matt had suggested "Leigh" with no alternate, and her mother thought she should be named after her dear sister, Emma, who died young. She had recently heard on the radio that Emma has become the most popular girl's name for a baby, so she thinks she has a "good case" for the name, Emma. Incidentally, they did have the ultrasound test, and the baby is definitely a girl. Suzanne hadn't decided yet how to completely ignore their preferences and name the baby, Lauren.

She discussed this with Jennie, and Jennie agreed that Suzanne has a problem. Jennie said "Your only solution is to name her Lauren Leigh. Tell your mother that you and Matt want the honor of naming your first child." Suzanne agreed – the baby will be Lauren Leigh Shapiro.

Suzanne and Jennie delighted in spending time together discussing every thing from prenatal yoga classes to intercourse after delivery. "We've been through so many stages. We've seen each other at our very best and less than our best. Over the years, we've developed a deep attachment, a real love and affection."

"Remember when we went to The Quorum after writing class and solved the world's problems, but not our own? It would be fun to go there sometime after Lauren is born. I wonder if Brian still owns it. Seeing us with children, he would probably think we were just dreamers then and now we are just typical housewives with children."

Jennie laughed, "Yes, you could tell him you published a book of poetry and you are president of Stein Injection Molding."

"And, I'll tell him you're a bestselling author with three books on the best seller list."

"Since my books have been published, I have heard from old friends and acquaintances telling me how they like my books, how little we really knew of each other when we were young, and they are happy for who I am now and my success. Their letters are so gratifying; they are the encouragement I need to continue."

"I can certainly appreciate that. Do you have another book in mind? Matt would love to hear that. Speaking of Matt – his birthday is next week, and I need to do some shopping. I don't like his underwear, I'd like to get him some Calvin Klein briefs – they are so sexy!"

"Tom wears Calvin's and likes them – so do I."

The following weekend, Suzanne woke during the night from painful contractions, and she immediately thought "this must be it!"

When they arrived at the hospital her contractions were eight minutes apart. Everything was proceeding normally, the contractions were closer together and, as instructed, she was pushing, then with more painful contractions, pushing harder and harder, but nothing was happening. They discovered the baby was stuck in the birth canal, and she had to push for three hours. Dr. Goldman ended up having to use the vacuum extractor to get the baby out. Finally, Suzanne gave birth to an eight and one-half pound baby girl shortly before noon. (As she described it later, they yanked the baby out causing tears which required stitches). She was completely exhausted and in considerable pain, but she had to know whether Lauren was okay. Dr. Goldman assured her the baby was perfect in every way.

Matt had been at her side throughout her ordeal, and Suzanne said, "We will only have one child."

"Darling, that's perfectly okay with me – we have a beautiful healthy baby, and I thank God for that."

After Suzanne recovered for two days, she went home and her loving parents couldn't do enough for her and the baby. They were thrilled with their granddaughter. She later would tell everyone Lauren was "very mature upon birth," - maybe the close association with her grandparents had something to do with it.

Lauren had Matt's brown hair and her mother's natural curl. Her head was covered with beautiful ringlets of brown hair and with her large brown eyes, she was adorable.

Suzanne's parents had sold their large home in Lake Forest, and they bought a condo in the same high rise where Suzanne and Matt lived.

Suzanne was anxious to go back to the office, and they were going to hire a nanny to come in and take care of Lauren, but her parents were horrified at such an idea. They would be the caretakers of their only grandchild, and so each day, Suzanne and Matt dropped Lauren off at their place while they went to work. Suzanne doesn't expect this arrangement to endure indefinitely, but she was happy with it while it would last.

Chapter Sixteen

Tom's classes adjourned until fall, and they were planning two weeks of fishing, hiking and swimming at a resort on Gull Lake in northern Minnesota. They decided the fishing cabin in the woods was too small and primitive for a small baby. This year, Tom's love of fishing and Jennie's love of writing will be enjoyed at the whim of Charlie.

His thoughts were centered on their vacation as he was driving his BMW along Lake Shore Drive when a car shot out in front of him from a side street. He tried to brake to a stop, the car did a figure eight, there was the screech of tires and the crash of crumpling metal as the two cars collided. Then all was silent for a while. All of a sudden, the earsplitting wail of several police sirens and flashing emergency lights followed by two ambulances broke the silence. When the paramedics saw that Tom wasn't moving and he appeared to be unconscious or dead, they rushed him to Northwestern Hospital where the doctors examined him for head injuries to determine the cause of his comatose condition. They did find some cranial swelling, but additional examinations and tests would be necessary. Miraculously, he didn't have any broken bones.

An ER staff nurse checked his ID for his next of kin and dialed his home number. When the phone rang, Jennie was expecting to hear Tom's voice, not the woman who asked, "Is this Mrs. Thomas Doyle?" And, then "there's been an accident and he's at Northwestern Hospital. I think you should come. He is still in ER; the doctors are worried about his brain."

Jennie was panic-stricken at hearing the nurse's diagnosis and abruptly stated, "I'll be there."

She called Denise and asked if she could stay with Charlie while she went to the hospital.

As Denise entered, Jennie was prepared to leave. It wasn't necessary to give her a lot of instructions; she has sat with Charlie on several occasions.

With heavy traffic, the drive to the hospital seemed like an eternity, and more than once Jennie sounded her horn. It was something she normally abhors doing, but at the moment, she felt her actions were justified. She parked her car and ran breathless to the entrance. Later she did not recall driving to the hospital, even starting the motor. Until she saw Tom, her mind seemed to have gone blank.

She asked for the Emergency Room, but was bewildered at the directions hurriedly given her. An older Asian-American woman looked at Jennie sympathetically, took her hand, led her to ER and directed her to Tom's room.

As she approached Tom's bed, she gasped in surprise. The raw scraped bruise on the left side of his face was a bloody red and a hideous purple and green. The doctor turned to her and, extending a hand, asked "Are you Mrs. Doyle?"

"Yes, I am; how is he?" as she returned his handshake.

"He is breathing on his own, but he is still unconscious. We did a head scan, but nothing shows positive. As you see, he is badly bruised on the left side of his face from his temple to his jaw. There's external swelling. He doesn't respond to light, pain or noise, which indicates there's internal swelling, too. We're monitoring for intracranial pressure. There's nothing at this point to suggest that we'll need to relieve it surgically. We'll be monitoring your husband to see if the pressure builds, then we stand a better chance of relieving it. The next 48 hours will be crucial. The good news is that what swelling there is now is minimal."

"Will there be permanent damage," Jennie asked. She needed to know just what to expect.

"I don't know."

"Does the chance of permanent damage increase the longer he is comatose?"

"Not if the swelling doesn't worsen."

"Is there anything you can do to get the swelling down?"

"He's on a drip to reduce it."

"What can I do to help?" Jennie asked.

"Not a whole lot. You can talk to him; some comatose patients are able to hear conversation, and he may respond. Once we make sure he is stable, we'll transfer him to NICU." He glanced at his watch and left.

Jennie took Tom's hand in hers and told him she loved him, and she would do everything she could to help him get better. She told him that Charlie misses his play time with him. She continued talking about things he would easily relate to, but there was no response.

She stared at him lying comatose unable to speak or smile, and she felt helpless and scared. The worst possibilities went through her mind. "What if he would have brain damage? What if he doesn't wake up? She thought, I've read about people being in comas for years before waking up. Some were normal and others had severe brain damage. What would I do if that happened? And what about Charlie, would he grow up with his father in an institution or in a nursing home?" Tears welled in her eyes, and she chastised herself for imagining the worst. "He will get well; we will get through this. If I tell him that often enough, he will."

She studied his face; he appeared to be in an innocent sleep. She patted his right cheek and lightly squeezed his hand – there was no response. She leaned over and kissed his forehead – there was no response.

She went out into the hallway and called Suzanne. While relating the day's events, her voice broke, but determining to be brave, she cleared her throat and continued talking. Suzanne asked what she and Matt could do, and Jennie told her at this time, there is nothing anybody can do. Maybe when Tom is moved from ER to NICU, she and Matt could visit him. The doctor said it would help to talk to him as some comatose patients could hear, and conversation may help him to respond.

Suzanne asked about his doctors, and Jennie told her they have the best neurologist in the city overseeing his treatment.

"What about Charlie? – who is with him?

"Denise is with him today, and she will stay with him for awhile tomorrow since its Sunday, but I don't know who I will get when she goes back to work on Monday."

"I know mom and dad could watch him for a while during the week. They adore Charlie, and Lauren sleeps most of the time. I know it wouldn't be a problem."

"Are you sure it wouldn't be too much for them at their age?"

"I'm certain it wouldn't – Charlie is a good baby. I'll talk to them and get back to you. In the meantime, we will pray for Tom. Tell him all his friends are praying for him."

When Jennie returned home she called the Police Department to find out where Tom's car was and called their insurance agent. He said he would go inspect the car and get back to her.

When she put Charlie to bed and went to bed herself, she had time to reflect on the day's happenings. "God only knows. He could wake up tonight. Or tomorrow. Or Monday. Or next week. This is bizarre. I know he will wake up, he's too healthy not to. We just have to take it one day at a time."

Sunday afternoon Denise came to stay with Charlie so she could go to the hospital for awhile. It was cute that Charlie actually greeted Denise with a big smile and waved his arms as though he was happy to see her. She knew that he likes her, and he didn't fuss at all when Jennie left.

When she arrived at Tom's bed, the nurse was making some adjustments with the drip and the overhead monitor, and Jennie asked if the drip was working. The nurse replied that it was even though the swelling hasn't come down; it hadn't increased, and that was very good. They are more concerned with the swelling increasing at this stage. She pointed to the monitor and told Jennie that his heartbeat is normal and steady – another good sign.

Jennie ran her fingers through Tom's hair, kissed his forehead and told him she loved him. Then she sat by the bed and told him everything that had happened. All his friends were concerned and they are praying for a speedy recovery. She told him Charlie misses him, and he was so happy to see Denise this morning that he didn't notice or care that she left.

She told him the nurse said that since the swelling hasn't increased, his condition was improving. Then she massaged his shoulders and stroked his arms and hands, the whole time talking to him. The nurse had told her she should continue to talk to him and to touch him as touching is a way to connect.

The nurse also told her comatose patients respond to smells, and if she has a perfume that Tom likes, she should wear it. He might respond to that. Jennie asked, "Do you think it will help?"

"It can't hurt," she replied.

Matt and Suzanne visited Tom often and went through the same routine of talking to him about anything and everything, even telling jokes, and holding his hands and caressing his arms, only to be saddened by a complete lack of response. When they questioned the nurses, they were told he could wake up in five minutes, five days, five weeks, or never. The doctors have no way of knowing. This was the first time they had been bluntly told "never," and his condition took on a whole new meaning. Thankfully, they had not been that blunt with Jennie.

They found it difficult to be optimistic with Jennie, but they continued to tell her, "he's healthy, he'll heal, he'll wake up any day now; it just takes awhile.

A few days later when Jennie walked into NICU, Tom's bed was empty, and it was made up for a new patient. She panicked, did his condition worsen, where is he? She found a nurse and asked, "Where's Mr. Doyle?"

"Oh, he was just taken to a patient room on the 2nd Floor. There's no reason for him to remain in NICU. We have done all we can do here. For now, it's just a matter of monitoring his vital signs and his progress. He and you will be more comfortable in a room."

She had mixed emotions – encouraged that he was out of Intensive Care, but afraid that there was nothing more that can be done for him. When she went to his room, the doctor dispelled her fears and told her that now his body has to take over and heal itself. They do not know how long this will take – each patient is different, but the healing process will take some time. He also told her she should continue to try to stimulate his senses through touch, sound and smell. Just continue as you have been doing.

Everything the doctor said seemed utterly banal and hopeless. One day a nurse asked, "How long can you keep this up – this constant daily vigil?"

Jennie replied, "As long as my husband needs me." Every day she watches for the flicker of an eyelid or the twitch of a hand.

It was two weeks ago when Tom went to Northwestern's Evanston campus for a business meeting. It was unusual to have a meeting on Saturday, but he didn't question it or wonder why. He was driving home on Lake Shore Drive when the car slammed into his driver's side and changed his life, possibly forever.

Jennie was at his bedside as she has been every day. On Saturdays and Sundays she is able to stay longer with Denise baby sitting. Due to their age, she doesn't want to stress Mr. and Mrs. Stein too much. They would never admit to Charlie being a burden, they want to do as much as they can for Jennie and Tom.

The nurse had just finished bathing Tom when she entered the room, and he was lying motionless on crisp, clean white sheets. The nurse nodded when Jennie entered, then moved about changing tubes and checking the IV drip. When she finished, Jennie asked if there had been any change in his condition. The nurse said the situation had not changed and left. Jennie leaned over to kiss him, and he smelled antiseptically clean. She took the tube of cream from her handbag and gently rubbed it into his skin, working carefully around the bruise on the left side of his face. The purple color was fading, and a sickening yellow-green-gold color appeared. It would be a long time before the bruise disappeared entirely. She picked up his hand that lay limp and studied his eyes for a sign of movement behind the lids. Seeing none, she looked up at the monitor, and his heart beat was still even as it has been for two weeks. It gives her assurance that he is definitely alive. The nurse returned, and Jennie asked if they had any idea when Tom would wake up, and she said, "We simply do not know, and the best I can say is that he is a good candidate for recovery."

Another day of hopelessness, and then the thought came to her that any day he could slide from this comatose state into his death, and she would never speak to him again. This has happened to others, and she recalled several years ago a friend relating a tragic family death. Her elderly father was walking to his car in a parking lot when he slipped on black ice, fell, and his head took the brunt of his fall on the asphalt. He immediately went into a comatose condition and remained in the coma for twenty days, then slipped from the coma to his death. During this time the family had remained at his bedside talking and doing all the things that Tom's doctor suggested to no avail. Situations such as this raced around and around in her mind, so she questioned each new nurse who comes on duty. Yesterday, the nurse said, "They generally wake up anywhere between two and four weeks." That has been the most encouraging advice she has received. Only time will tell, there is still hope.

Rev. Paul Robinson visited every week and left his card on the bedside table. Even though Jennie and Tom attend Sunday services sporadically, he was there for them with his thoughts and prayers.

The following day Jennie was driving the familiar route to the hospital and parking in the same high-rise garage to take her place at Tom's bedside. She was talking to him as usual, and she leaned over and kissed his cheek. While she was close to his face, she thought she saw the eyelid on his right eye open and then it quickly closed. She almost let out a cry of surprise, but waited for another movement. Nothing happened. She went to the door and summoned a nurse in the hallway. "I know I saw his right eyelid open and then close, but there hasn't been any movement since."

"It could very well be that he is in the process of waking – a patient doesn't just wake up and remain alert, it's a gradual process. Another movement may not happen until tomorrow. But now that there is a sign of waking, we will monitor him and watch him more closely. You did the right thing in telling me about the slightest change."

Jennie was elated and went in and kissed Tom good-bye and told him she would be back tomorrow.

When she picked up Charlie at the Stein's, she told them what had happened. They were certain he would wake any day now. She called Suzanne and related the good news. Suzanne said they were planning to stop and see Tom on their way home from work tonight. Suz said they would watch him closely.

The next day Jennie greeted Tom with a kiss and said, "Hi, how are you" hoping for a response, but there was nothing. A doctor wearing green scrubs came in and checked his monitor for vital signs, and Jennie asked "Isn't there anything more that can be done?" She pressured the doctors and nurses, trying to manage the situation, hoping for encouraging answers.

"Not yet. The fact that he's not getting worse is good."

"You people all say that, but that's not encouraging, a coma seems one step removed from death."

"I know it seems that way to you, but to us it's standard with head injuries. I have a very positive feeling that your husband will come out of it soon."

Jennie was at home playing with Charlie when the phone rang. Lately, the ringing of the phone both alarmed and excited her knowing that it may be a call from the hospital. This time it was the hospital, and the nurse was calling to tell her that her husband had opened his eyes and looked around bewildered. He glanced around the room as if he was looking for something or someone in particular, and then closed his eyes. She said "I'm certain he was looking for you, Mrs. Doyle." His vital signs are all still very good, so we are certain his health is good except for losing weight. After all, he was in a coma for eighteen days without food except for the IV. We will be watching him closely throughout the night. I just thought you should know. Tomorrow you may have a wonderful surprise."

She called Suzanne; they will definitely visit him tomorrow. Jennie hardly slept that night thinking about Tom's reaction today when he looked around, and she wasn't there. She will make it up to him tomorrow.

She felt a rush of adrenaline and sense of anticipation as she drove to the hospital. The nightmare of the last few weeks was over, and she was anxious to see how Tom would react to her and his surroundings after being in a coma for eighteen days.

When she arrived at his room, she was met by a man delivering a huge bouquet of balloons. The card read, "Welcome Home – We Love You," Suzanne and Matt. She smiled and thought, "Yes, welcome home, Tom." Tom smiled as best he could in his weakened condition when she approached his bed and kissed him all over his face. He put his arms around her, and they were interrupted when two male nurses appeared with a gurney and announced that they had to take him to X-Ray for a scan of his head to make sure everything is okay.

His doctor entered the room, and Jennie asked, "Is he out of the coma free and clear?"

"It took eighteen days for him to heal enough to regain consciousness, so we expect him to remain conscious. If the scan is positive and we don't see anything wrong he will be okay. We'll continue with meds for awhile to minimize the chance of the swelling returning. Aside from that, we expect he will be fine."

"What about food, when can he have something to eat?" she asked.

"We'll start him on a liquid diet and then gradually go to soft solids. Tomorrow we'll get him out of bed and on his feet. We want him eating and walking. Once he has accomplished that and he has regained full function of his bowels, he's all yours."

Jennie was overjoyed, "How many days will that take?"

"Three days should do it – he should be home by Sunday."

The doctor added, "He's lucky if there is such a thing as good luck in his case – considering what otherwise could have gone wrong – he's very lucky."

"Yes, when I think that he might never have regained consciousness, he is lucky it was only eighteen days."

Tom was wheeled back into the room, and he seemed surprised as they brought him into the room. He asked Jennie, "Why am I here?"

"Don't you remember the accident? You were in a bad car accident, and you have been in a coma for eighteen days."

"I don't remember an accident, and I can't believe I have been lying here for eighteen days," and he closed his eyes.

"It's too much activity too soon," she thought, and it was time for her to leave so she kissed him on the forehead and told him she would return tomorrow.

The next morning when she visited Tom, the first thing she noticed was that his IV pole was gone. His breakfast tray held a small bowl of broth and a dish of red Jello. He was drinking a glass of juice.

"How are you feeling?" Jennie asked as she smiled and bent to kiss him.

"Better," he said, but I wish I could make some sense of all this and remember what happened and why I'm here."

Before Jennie could explain, the doctor entered and told him that when he finished his breakfast, "I want you to take a walk down the hall. A therapist will take you." He looked at his half-eaten breakfast tray and remarked, "You ate. Good. We have to fatten you up a little. The more you eat and the more you walk, the stronger you'll be and the faster your plumbing will start up again. As soon as that happens, the sooner you can go home."

The therapist came, put the therapy belt around his waist and helped him to his feet. With Jennie at his other side, he walked slowly concentrating on the floor in front of them and counting each of the black and white linoleum squares as if they were a measure of distance. When they reached the end, the therapist said, "You're doing great." By the time he was back in his room, he had broken into a sweat and was breathing hard. Jennie helped him into bed and asked if he needed anything. Exhausted, he shook his head and closed his eyes.

Jennie kissed him goodbye and left, "It's going to take some time for him to regain his strength; he's been through an ordeal. I know he will be stronger tomorrow."

Chapter Seventeen

You never know when something is going to happen to change your life. You are never prepared. Your life can end in an instant. Those thoughts went through Tom's mind as he lay in bed trying to piece his life together. He remembered going to the Evanston campus for a meeting and returning home by way of Lake Shore Drive as he had done so often in the past. He remembered driving, but he didn't remember the accident that Jennie said totaled his BMW. Everyone tells him he has been in a coma for eighteen days, but he only recalls driving down Lake Shore Drive. He can't quite phantom losing eighteen days of his life.

"Good morning," the nurse cheerily called out as she entered carrying his breakfast tray. He straightened up and lifted the metal cover hiding another bowl of broth and gazed at the green Jello. He turned his head and slumped back in the bed.

"Not hungry?" she asked. "If you eat your liquids again today, tomorrow we will start your solids diet. After breakfast, the therapist will take you for a walk," and she left.

When Jennie arrived, the therapist was returning Tom to his room, and she noticed he was walking steadier today. His legs looked thinner, but she didn't comment. Tom said that his legs felt a little stronger after walking today. The therapist told him she would return after lunch, and they would go for another walk. He lay back into the bed with a sigh as if he was exhausted.

Jennie told him they received a check from the insurance company and now he can go shopping for a new car. "She asked, "Do you feel nervous about being in a car after the accident?"

"I don't remember the accident." Changing the subject, he asked about Charlie and commented, "I wondered if he has grown in eighteen days."

"I think you will see a difference – he's putting on weight, and he wants to sit up by himself. It seems that every day he does something different."

"I'm anxious to see him. What day is it?"

"It's Friday – if you eat solid food tomorrow and have a bowel movement, the doctor said you can go home on Sunday. That's what I am planning on."

"I hope so, too. I can't believe I have just been lying here motionless for eighteen days! I'll have to get out and do some jogging. My legs are really weak. It will take some time to get back in shape."

"I'll be glad when you come home. I felt so helpless coming here to visit you when you were non-responsive. I talked to you and massaged your arms and shoulders, but it didn't do any good. And then I would think what would I do if you didn't wake up? The longer it went on, the more afraid I was. Eighteen days is a long time."

"You're telling me! I've been thinking about it a lot. Honey, we have a lot of making up to do."

"Who is watching Charlie today?" he asked.

"The Steins have him so I can't stay long. I worry that with Lauren, Charlie is a burden to them at their ages. Lauren is changing a lot – she's going to be a beautiful child.

"Well, she has good looking parents so she has a lot going for her."

"The plumbing's working!" That was Tom's greeting to Jennie when she arrived Sunday morning. She went to his bedside and kissed him on the cheek. He put his arms around her and drew her close.

"Ahem," The doctor cleared his throat again before entering. "Sorry to interrupt you two, but we have busy schedules around here."

Tom laughed and said, "That's okay, Doc. Have you heard the news?"

"If you are referring to your bowel movement, yes, that's why I'm here. I'll check you over and go over the records of your vitals, and if everything is in order, you can leave this afternoon. A nurse will discharge you." He drew the curtain, and Jennie left the room to call Suzanne and Matt. She was anxious to tell them the good news.

The nurse wheeled Tom down the corridor to the elevator. Jennie remarked, "Do you realize that I have taken this same elevator every day for almost three weeks. It's a relief to know that today is the last day. Now we can get on with our lives."

Jennie brought the car to the door, and Tom asked if she wanted him to drive. She had wondered if he would be apprehensive about driving, but, of course, he doesn't remember the accident or the coma so he doesn't have any fears to overcome. She moved to the passenger seat.

Charlie's eyes lit up like a pinball machine when Tom picked him up and hugged him. Clearly, he missed his daddy.

Tom went to his desk and was astounded to see the piles of mail neatly sorted into categories unknown as yet. He stood staring, and Jennie gently reminded him, "It was eighteen days." No doubt there will be other incidents or reminders of the lost days in his life. He picked up the pink "While You Were Out" slips and leafed through them studying each one carefully. He quickly scanned the envelopes, advertising brochures, and other junk mail, and tossed them aside. He was not in the mood for any of this.

Then he noticed the stack of cards Jennie had put off to the side. He thumbed through them scanning the return addresses. Recognizing names, he surmised the entire Kellogg faculty received word of the accident and were sending their get-well wishes. He tossed them back on the pile; they too can wait.

He walked into the kitchen, dumped his tepid coffee, and poured a fresh cup. He had been doing that for the past hour, never actually drinking it. Jennie knew it was too soon for him to concentrate and think clearly. "Honey, its Sunday, why don't you relax today. It's a nice sunny afternoon, let's put Charlie in the stroller and go for a short walk. We can both use some exercise."

The following day Tom took a deep breath and finally turned his attention to the disarray of papers littering his desk. He decided he could no longer ignore the mail that may need some action from him. He briefly looked through the envelopes, and then hurriedly opened the letter from his publisher, Northwestern University Press, which stated, "In response to a flurry of orders from chain and independent bookstores and wholesalers, we are delighted to inform you that we are going to reprint an additional 1,000 copies of your book, "The Economic Growth of China." It went on to say "the book has garnered an enthusiastic early response…the first edition had a 5,000 copy printing…"

"Jennie, Jennie, come here." Jennie took the letter that he thrust in her hands, read it, and threw her arms around him stating, "You are a noted author…you will no doubt be invited to speaking engagements at various venues, possibly even be asked to appear on TV and radio talk shows."

"Don't get carried away. I haven't had any publicity yet. But I am pleased with the response…I wasn't expecting that."

"I see the beginning of a new career when you retire from teaching. It's done all the time; someone leaves a position and the first thing they do is write a book!"

"Well, it's something to consider. When I have a genuine interest in a subject, it isn't an effort to write about it. I rather like being on a soapbox."

"We'll become a family of authors; I'll write fiction, and you'll write non-fiction." She lovingly messed his hair and said, "I have work to do" and left.

Included in the stack of mail was a brochure advertising the resort and cabins on Gull Lake where they were planning to return for a vacation. They have reservations for two weeks in August, and it is rapidly approaching. He put the brochure off to the side.

They had decided to look for a new car after lunch, and he went on-line to look at current BMW models. After looking at the various cars, he opted to duplicate the model he had which was totaled in the crash. It had everything he liked and needed so why not stay with it.

Charlie had been bathed, clothed and fed, and now it was play time. Tom put him on the rug and encouraged him to crawl and stand while he held on to him. Charlie's legs were getting stronger, and he liked to put his weight on them and attempt to walk. Most of all, he liked the attention his daddy gave him.

Tom's legs are still weak from being immobile for eighteen days, and while eating lunch they decided to go for a leisurely walk after getting the car. It was a delightful early summer day, and the lake was beckoning. He wanted to get back into his exercise routine. He can't help but think about waking up in the hospital but not remembering the accident that put him there. Jennie is seriously contemplating using the situation as the subject for her next novel; the protagonist will also be a man who is injured and becomes comatose.

The month of July flew by, and the hot, humid days of August drove everyone to their lake cottages, eager to escape the sweltering city. Jennie and Tom joined the exodus of vacationers heading to northern Minnesota where they vacationed before they were married. Tom loved to fish, and Gull Lake is noted for its many walleye, northern and bass. Tom loved the sport of fishing and most often caught and released them after he has brought home a catch for dinner.

This vacation would be a complete break from her writing discipline, however, even while on the road, out of habit, she found herself taking notes and writing segments of her fourth book, **The Man of her Dreams.** Her mind was always attuned to writing, and she worked with dogged intensity on a book once it came together in her mind.

It was a long drive from Chicago, but they stopped fairly often for Tom and Charlie to stretch their legs. Tom was still recovering, and Charlie needed a change of position from his car seat. Jennie was surprised that he slept as much as he did. Evidently, the smooth motion of the car cruising the expressways soothed and lulled him to sleep.

Alfalfa fields blurred past and fields golden with dandelions disappeared as they left the Interstate and turned onto the two-lane county road. Tom slowed as the road narrowed and gently zigzagged through the woods leading to the lake. They circled the lake and followed the frontage road to their lake-view cabin nestled among tall pines just a block from the main Lodge with its fine dining and nightly entertainment. The paved road meandered past the swimming pool, and Tom noticed the dock and fishing boats were just steps away from their cabin.

While unpacking the car, Tom commented "One would think that a baby would travel light, but I think Charlie's stuff out-weighs my luggage and my fishing gear combined."

Jennie laughed, "I know what you mean – his clothes and paraphernalia practically filled the trunk. His diapers alone take up a lot of space. After we unpack, let's walk up to the Lodge and get something to eat – I don't feel like cooking tonight."

"I second that! I think I'll unwind with a Scotch first."

Monday was a beautiful day, and Tom got up early and was out on the lake fishing before Jennie got Charlie bathed and fed. She took a sip of the coffee he had made and grimaced. It was cold and strong so she made a fresh pot. It was brewing as Tom entered with a good-sized northern which would be their dinner tonight. After breakfast, they put Charlie in the stroller and proceeded to the jogging path for some walking exercise. Then she put him down for a nap and, they went out on their private dock for swimming and sunning. They liked the privacy of their well-equipped cottage even though they had neighbors on either side. Later they would call on them and introduce themselves deciding that it's a good idea to know who your neighbors are when you're out in the woods.

After they finished a late dinner of fresh fried fish, a bolt of lightning flashed through the sky and they heard distant rumbles of thunder. As Tom commented, "I hope it's just a quick shower," it slowly started to rain and then increased to torrents. The rain thrashed relentlessly at the windows, and thunder roared as the heavens opened up. Lightning became spectacular and frightening as it lit up the room.

Tom and Jennie poured a glass of wine and tried to become interested in TV, but the picture flip-flopped with each bolt of lightning. Then the overhead lights flickered and went out, and the room was bathed in darkness except for intervals of lightning flashes lighting up the room. Tom put his arm around Jennie and kissed her gently. They sat quietly snuggling and kissing expecting the lights to return, but sensing that was not going to happen, they felt their way to the bedroom.

It was still raining when they awoke, but the electricity was working. Tom looked longingly at the boat moored to the dock and sighed. Now the rain was streaking down the windows in sheets that obliterated the view of the lake. He picked up the textbook he brought along in the event of rain and leafed through a few pages with feigned interest, then abruptly closed it and put it aside.

Jennie appeared saying, "I think he will have a long nap this afternoon, he is really tired. Shall we play gin rummy or just talk? I remember Lynn and I used to while away long afternoons by asking each other to relate different events in our lives. For instance, "What was the silliest thing you did in your youth?"

Tom thought for a moment and said, "I needed a job during Christmas break, and the only job I could find was playing a department store elf. I had no idea what an elf was supposed to do. They told me to be active and animated – I was there to amuse children and get laughs. Well, it wasn't difficult for me to make a fool of myself; I had a fair amount of experience doing that while growing up. Until I realized that my education was an investment in the future, I thought I was the class clown.

"That's really funny; I would never expect that of you — it's a side of you I don't know. You learned an important lesson at the right time in your life. Okay, now your next question is what was the saddest event in your young life?"

"It has to be when my father died. We did everything together, and I idolized him. He was a fighter pilot during the war, and I never tired of the stories he told me over and over. He was proud of his role in WWII, and I worshipped him not only as my father, but as a war hero. I treasure having his Silver Star, Distinguished Flying Cross, and the Air Medal with two Oak Leaf Clusters. I want Charlie to have them eventually. When Dad died, initially I lost my purpose in life, but the memory of our happy lives together inspired me to follow in his footsteps. I wanted to be just like him."

"Okay, now it's your turn. What was the silliest thing you did?"

"I guess it has to be the day I played beauty shop with my dolls. I had three dolls with long hair, and I lined them up in my make-believe beauty shop and proceeded to cut their hair short. When mother saw what I had done, she said, 'You know their hair will not grow back.' Realizing what I had done, I cried and cried. Mother and father tried to console me by telling me they liked them better with short hair."

"That certainly was a bittersweet lesson!"

"Like you, the saddest time of my young life was losing my father suddenly due to a heart attack. He died too young, and it was very difficult for mother. She mourned him for a long time. I went away to college so my studies kept me from dwelling on it, but she was home alone, and it was a difficult time for her. Isn't it unusual that we both lost our fathers when we were young."

Jennie stated, "Okay, now for your last question, who's your favorite cartoon character?"

Tom said, "You probably think its Charlie Brown, but my favorite was Dick Tracy. He was a hard-hitting, fast-shooting police detective who successfully tracked down gangsters in Chicago, and his cases usually ended in a shootout. He couldn't have tracked them down without his ingenious two-way wrist radio. I remember characters like Shoulders, Pruneface, and Flattop Jones. Flattop came close to killing Tracy, but, of course, that couldn't happen. I remember his girlfriend, Tess Truehart. She jilted him and married someone else. What was your favorite?"

"Well, my favorite cartoon was Peanuts although we always called it Charlie Brown. The cartoon was ahead of its time because of Franklin and the fact that there were three girls on Charlie's baseball team. That was revolutionary. My favorite character was Lucy. It was really funny when she held the football for Charlie to kick and then at the last minute she would pull the ball away as he was kicking. Then Charlie, being off balance, would sail into the air and land on his back with a loud thud. But she was mean to her brother, Linus; that I didn't like."

"Look, the rain has stopped," Tom said, "And I hear Charlie; he's awake. I think I'll take the boat out and see if I can catch something for dinner tonight."

Even though he returned empty-handed, he was smiling. "I have been talking with our neighbors, and they want us to come over for a drink. Afterward, we'll go to the Lodge for dinner."

"That sounds fun – I had better change clothes."

"You look great, and I might add 'sexy'. You don't have to change. You're wearing jeans and a T-shirt. If you stood in front of your closet for four hours that's precisely what you'd come up with."

"Since you put it that way, I won't change a thing. But I'll check Charlie to make sure he's dry and then I'll be ready."

As they were walking to the neighbor's cabin, Tom said, "They are from Chicago, and their names are Paul and Ann Blair – they are nice people."

After introductions, it was Charlie who took center stage. Ann told them she was four months pregnant, and they are expecting their first child. Charlie liked the attention she lavished on him, and he responded in kind. Tom had a rapport with Paul and Ann as they are both school teachers.

As Tom and Jennie left the Lodge and walked the cedar path through the tall pines toward home, it started to rain, and not being able to do anything about it, they laughed as the heavens opened and the rain turned into a soft, cleansing shower.

The next morning was gray and overcast. Jennie woke early and moaned, "Another rainy day." Charlie had the same sentiment and began to cry. She ran to pick him up before he woke Tom. She removed his soaked diaper, and he cooed and smiled. She thought, "I hope my precious little boy never loses his zest for living!" She showered and dressed and when she returned to the bedroom, Charlie was in bed with Tom, and they were sleeping soundly. Evidently, Charlie had begun to cry and Tom got up and put him in their bed.

She went to the kitchen and made a pot of coffee. The aroma drifted to the bedroom, and Tom appeared in the doorway carrying a smiling, happy little boy. She poured some coffee and remarked, "We should have brought some games." Charlie reminded her that he was again wet and hungry, and she commented, "After I bath and feed Charlie, let's make a big breakfast."

"Sounds great," Tom said, and he headed for the shower.

The smell of breakfast bacon lingered with the lake smells coming through the screen door. While they were enjoying coffee, the rain stopped so they put Charlie in the stroller and went for a walk along the lake as the water lapped at the shore. Even though it was August, it seemed like the first day of autumn with a smattering of orange and red leaves glowing in the sunlight.

"What is that noise; is it a bird?" Jennie asked.

"That's a loon; Minnesota is known for its large loon populations – in fact, it's the state bird."

"I don't think Illinois has loons; I've never heard of them there. They must be native to the northern lake regions."

"Yes, they are, and it's against the law to kill a loon. The noise that sounds like a hoot is used to

209

communicate among each other, and the long, haunting sound is their wail. The wail is used to call back and forth so they know where they are relative to each other. They have a sophisticated communication system."

That evening the wailing and hooting of the loons lulled them to sleep.

When they returned to Chicago, they learned that Suzanne's father, Ben Stein, had another stroke which was fatal, and he died instantly. They didn't get back in time for the funeral, but they would sit shivah. Jennie is familiar with many Jewish traditions, and she explained the tradition of shivah to Tom.

The following day they went to the Stein's home to sit shivah and mourn with Suzanne and her family. Suzanne greeted them, and they hugged and softly sobbed, agreeing "there are no words." In keeping with custom, they had removed their leather shoes before entering, and they wore a torn black ribbon as an expression of sympathy. They brought some fresh kosher bread from the bakery to share with others. She noticed the memorial candle that will glow brightly throughout the week.

Mrs. Stein was holding up well with sympathy and support from her family and long-time friends. So many people from Mr. Stein's business came to lend their support to her and Suzanne. After visiting and properly expressing their condolences, Jennie and Tom quietly left.

Now Suzanne was truly at the helm of Stein Injection Molding. Initially, she missed her father's presence if she wanted advice on a business matter, but she quickly discovered her intuition was the proper course of action.

Not only did her responsibilities increase at the office, she had to minister to her mother who was having difficulty accepting the loss of her husband and was terribly lonely. Suzanne wanted to spend more time with Lauren to bond as a mother and daughter should. Lauren was at the stage of development when she wanted and needed her mother. Matt tried to be a full time parent and an assistant to her in the business. It was a difficult time for both Suzanne and Matt. Jennie wanted to help them, and she was eager to care for Lauren whenever possible. Charlie was intrigued with Lauren and liked having her around.

Jennie had taken Charlie for a walk, and as she was returning someone was erecting a "For Sale" sign in front of the duplex next to theirs. She and Tom had discussed their need for additional space since Charlie was born, but they disliked the thought of moving from their prime location in Lincoln Park. She asked the man about the property being for sale, and he said he was only hired to put up the sign and didn't know anything about the property. She wrote down the name and phone number on the sign and went inside. Tom had told her after she first met him that he wished he could own both units. He was apprehensive about living so close to future occupants who might not be desirable neighbors. She looked at her watch and since Tom would be in a class, she decided the good news would have to wait until he arrived home.

Tom returned home in an exuberant mood, and Jennie knew he had seen the For Sale sign. He had also jotted down the name and phone number on the sign. He put down his brief- case, took off his jacket, and dialed the number. Jennie heard him ask, "Could we look at it tonight," and the reply was affirmative. He ended the conversation saying, "We'll see you at seven."

Over dinner, they discussed the renovation and which walls would need to be knocked down. Jennie asked, "Have you ever seen the inside of that unit?"

"No, I haven't – I'm just assuming the floor plan is the same as ours. We could open up each kitchen into one large room with duplicate appliances and space for two cooks to function independently. The small living rooms would become one large drawing room with two fireplaces. With its imposing limestone facade, this building could become just another of Lincoln Park's stately, early twentieth-century mansions."

"Sounds very costly and time-consuming," Jennie stated.

"Not really – but it depends upon the condition of that unit. They are both well-dressed, professional people, so I'm sure their home is a reflection of themselves. If the bedrooms and bathrooms are in good condition, that portion wouldn't be costly – mostly decorating."

Ginny, the real estate representative, was on time, and they went next door. Tom and Jennie have known the middle-aged couple who live there, but had not been inside their home. They are moving as a result of his business transfer to Washington, D.C. which they both look forward to. Entering the duplex, they were assaulted by a riot of flowery pink chintz. "Oh, how lovely," Jennie remarked. Tom grimaced at the extravagance of the décor and her remark. The Hayward's said they would be willing to consider a good offer, and they liked the idea of one person owning the whole house and restoring it to its former glory. Tom and Jennie were overjoyed, and Tom made an offer.

Chapter Eighteen

e may be crazy, but this place is going to be the home of our dreams – it will be the showcase of Lincoln Park." Jennie was daydreaming again instead of writing another chapter to her book.

Ever since Tom made an offer on the duplex next door, she has not been able to concentrate on her writing or anything else except Charlie, who is impossible to overlook.

After a week of anxiety, Tom was told the Hayward's next door accepted his offer. Mr. Hayward is a political analyst, and he was anxious to move and begin his new position in Washington, D.C. They did not want any problems with their relocation.

Tom had done some research before considering this project. He discovered that under current zoning laws duplexes are no longer allowed, and single-family homes sell for more money than duplexes even though they have the same, or more, square footage. He thought he could make some money by converting the duplex into a single family home. First, he needed to meet with the zoning committee and then have floor plans drawn up. All this would take time, and it would probably be close to spring before the project got underway.

Thanksgiving Day was rapidly approaching, and Lynn and Roger invited them to come to Quincy. They eagerly accepted their invitation; Tom likes Lynn and Roger and he likes the tranquil rural drive to Quincy. The day was nothing out of the ordinary when they left Chicago, but as soon as they left the city limits heading south it began to snow lightly. An hour later the large, leisurely flakes turned to smaller and denser flakes, and Tom and Jennie knew they were really in for it. The wind picked up speed and the snow began to slant down heavier and harder, and soon small drifts of snow spread across the highway. The tires scrunched as they drove through the drifts. The wind continued to howl and moan, and their conversation turned to silence as Tom kept both hands on the steering wheel as the windshield wipers struggled to keep the windows clear. Jennie tried to gauge the heaviness of the snow by counting how many telephone poles she could see behind her. Four, then three, then two – and when the wind gusted again, the telephone pole they just passed vanished from sight.

Out the front window, the highway ahead stretched into view and in the next instant it vanished. Tom slowed the car from 65 to 60, to 50, and to 45. Once, as a gust of wind came suddenly, the road momentarily disappeared, and the tires on the right side crunched on the snow and gravel on the shoulder. Tom quickly got the car back, but he said, "Maybe I should stay there. The traction's better."

By now the highway was becoming snow-packed and glazed. Jennie asked, "Do you think this will let up soon?"

"Are you kidding?" Tom replied, "Blizzards in the country can last for days."

Jennie leaned forward and peered out the windshield as though all it took to see through the blinding snow was concentration. "Of course, it blows like this in the country, there isn't anything between here and Canada to stop the wind. But the summers are nice."

"Yeah, Tom said scornfully, "It gets hot and sticky, and the mosquitoes are big enough to carry you away." (She could tell the pressure from driving was getting to him). He stopped talking and slowed as a truck going by in the other lane threw up so much snow he was temporarily blinded.

For a time the storm lessened, and some distance was given back to them. Tom speeded up, trying to travel as many miles as he could to make up for lost miles. Then, on a straightaway and without warning, the car's rear end slid across the middle line. Suddenly the car was spinning around and they were facing the direction from which they just came. It happened too quickly to be frightened and there they were, sitting on the shoulder facing in the opposite direction, back toward Chicago.

After a silence, Tom said, "It's a good thing no cars were coming."

Jennie's head was bowed, and her hands had covered her eyes. Then, turning around to check on Charlie, who was sleeping peacefully oblivious to the raging storm, she said, "I don't want to go any farther."

Tom said, "We can't just sit here – we'll stop at the first town we come to."

"No, said Jennie, "Let's just wait here for awhile until the storm let's up."

"It's not going to let up, it's only going to get worse. We've got to get someplace while we can. It's dangerous to stay here; another car might not see us and plow right into us. We could get drifted in here and not get out." There was silence, and then he added, "We might run out of gas and freeze to death."

"You're right, Jennie replied, "We have to keep going.
Tom carefully turned the car around and drove on though at a slower speed. After driving for

about a half hour, the snow began to abate, and as they neared Quincy, it cleared up completely. As they drove into town the sun came out, but not enough to melt all the snow from their vehicle, and Lynn and Roger were surprised to see their snow-covered car. It had not snowed in Quincy, and it was forecast that the storm would miss their area as it was headed north to Chicago.

They welcomed the warmth and smell of turkey roasting in the oven. The delicious aroma permeated the house. Lynn and Roger couldn't believe how much Charlie has grown. "He's two years old now, and he's into everything; always in motion. The only time we have a moment's peace is when he takes a nap."

Charlie became preoccupied with the toys Jennie brought along for him, and Tom and Roger sat down for a discussion while Jennie and Lynn brought dinner to the table. Of course, the dinner conversation centered around the duplex conversion. Roger asked about the problem of two front doors, and Tom told him they were fortunate that the attractive limestone façade has just one entrance. Inside there is an entrance hall with doors off of that so the facade will not have to be altered.

He told them the major renovation projects will include new walls, doors, plumbing, wiring and painting. Since each unit has three bedrooms and two baths, the completed home will have six bedrooms and four baths. The two downstairs bedrooms would be used as offices so that Tom and Jennie would each have an office. We may be knee-deep in construction debris for awhile, but it will be worth it.

Tom told them he got the duplex at a good price since the price of a duplex is often based on its income, and also they are difficult to sell since most people didn't want to be landlords or live that closely to a neighbor. This is especially true in the Lincoln Park area.

"You probably think we are crazy," Tom remarked.

"No, you are the sanest people I know. You will need additional insurance, you know!"

"Yes, that occurred to me. Write it up, Roger, and I'll take a look at it. We need to have everything covered while the workmen are there."

They gratefully accepted Lynn and Roger's kind invitation to spend the night. The next morning they were enroute to Chicago, squinting as they tried to shut out the blinding light that reflected off the dazzling white on white landscape that stretched for miles on every side of them. They mostly drove in silence that was not strained but comfortable. They were happy to be going home.

For Jennie, the month of November brought other memories. Even though she and Tom are endlessly happy and their lives are fulfilled, Jennie often thinks of Steve. She still struggles to come to terms with his death. She has gotten through the depression of grief, but she still suffers from feelings of guilt, and she needs to know the truth about his death, so she can somehow erase the guilt she has because of her high school reunion. She continued to communicate with Steve's parents and has learned many details of the on-going investigations surrounding his murder, however, his parents have mourned and prayed for guidance and now want to leave the matter in the past and not live their remaining years with an "open wound." They have been able to overcome their grief and have found closure to his death. Jennie wants the same, but she won't have closure until she learns all the details surrounding his death. Jim and Grace Hollis are sympathetic to her feelings and want to help her as much as possible so they continue to keep her informed of the local investigative work even though it tears their heartstrings.

Christmas was approaching, and Jennie was caught up in a shopping frenzy. For Tom, she selected a gray sports coat and coordinating shirt, tie, and slacks to add to his professional wardrobe. Charlie will get some toys, and a red sweater. Her favorite children's shop had traditional green Wellington rain boots for toddlers, and she couldn't resist them. He will be able to wear them in the spring when rain is plentiful.

Both Jennie and Tom love Christmas; the decorations and the music, and the wonderful smells of the kitchen. Last year's open house party was so successful they want to continue it year after year. The invitations are ready to mail, the aroma of Christmas cookies mingled with the aroma of fresh pine boughs and the sharp fragrance of Poinsettia's. Jennie is caught up in the traditions of Christmas that go back to her youth in Quincy. Tom will string the lights on the tree just as her father did before him, and she will carefully decorate the tree with her mother's prized ornaments. They are creating their own Christmas traditions now.

Tom and some fellow staff members volunteered to play Santa at a day care center in a housing project in Chicago. They provided Christmas cheer for sixty-five children, He said it was the most meaningful thing he has done in a long time. They all vowed to do it again next year.

The Northwestern Kellogg Business School staff party was again the highlight of the holiday season. It's such a festive and elegant affair, they would not want to miss it.

The Christmas Day service fell on a Sunday this year, and because of Charlie they attended that service instead of the Christmas Eve services. They had a leisurely breakfast and read the paper, then went to the eleven a.m. service. They planned a late dinner for just the two of them.

For New Year's Eve, Suzanne and Matt invited a few friends in for a casual dinner. Most of Matt's friends are writers and artists and, and when their lively conversation allowed, they played gin rummy. At the stroke of midnight, glasses clinked as they shared champagne toasts to the New Year. It was the perfect way to end another wonderful year.

On Saturday mornings, Tom woke up at ungodly hours. He liked to catch the 6 a.m. news while munching on a bowl of cereal, and then he went for a morning run. He jokingly tells everyone, "Jennie gets up at the crack of noon." Jennie wanted to join him some day; she needs to get back in shape. Before Charlie, they jogged together on Saturdays, and then stopped at the café down the street for hot meat loaf sandwiches on white bread with ketchup. After exercising in the cool morning air, they tasted heavenly.

Chapter Nineteen

*A*nyone wanting directions to 1932 Lakeview Avenue, was told "it's the limestone building with the two dumpsters on the front lawn." The renovation had begun in earnest, and they quickly realized what they were in for with a toddler underfoot. "No, Charlie, you can't play outside with all that debris lying around. Maybe your daddy will take you to the park."

From his perch on the ladder, Tom gave her a "you've got to be kidding look" and continued painting the ceiling. The painter that the sub-contractor lined up for painting wouldn't be available for two weeks. "I can do a lot of painting in two weeks," Tom declared. He is on summer vacation so he has the time.

Their morning routine was to get up early and have breakfast before the carpenters and the plumber arrive, and one morning as they staggered into the kitchen to make coffee, the room went dark. They tried all the light switches to no avail, the power was gone. A quick call was made to the electrician, and two hours later coffee was brewing. As they shared breakfast, they debated whether they would be able to stay in the house. The alternative of going to a motel or hotel was so dismal, they decided to stick it out even if it meant taking sponge baths and calling for pizza.

Suzanne was fascinated with the renovation project, as she is extremely interested in design and interior decorating, and she stopped by often to check on the project. She is intrigued with the "marriage" of the two units into its original design and floor plan. At her insistence, the beautiful crown molding in all rooms is being carefully preserved and will be put back in place.

She was certain that several rooms were formerly servant's quarters. One aspect of the project that they collaborated on was the new staircase to the second floor. It is an elegant staircase that curved up from the living room, and its placement created much debate between the two couples before plans could be finalized.

On another occasion, Tom and Jennie and Suzanne and Matt were sitting around discussing furniture for the "great room" as the living room was now referred due to its immense size. Jennie wanted the living room with its two fireplaces to be elegant, but not a gorgeous space that one felt compelled to walk by. She and Tom like to entertain, but they have a young child to consider.

Tom said, "There are two things every home must have – a comfortable reading chair and a table to put your drink on."

"Here, here," Matt remarked as he raised his glass.

Tom continued, "I want to have a wine cellar – not a ridiculously expensive one - just good wines to have on hand and drink over time so I can be a generous host, and we can have great parties."

The entrance hall now had French doors leading to the immense living room, and this room would be the heart and soul of the house. Jennie and Suzanne selected a wallpaper mural with an ocean view to emulate Lake Michigan for one wall in the dining room. Included on the first floor are the living and dining rooms, huge gourmet kitchen, breakfast room, bathroom, and his and hers offices. The fireplaces in the living room would not be altered. They like to entertain but prefer to do it on a casual level and a fireplace provides great ambience while friends and family hung out.

Upstairs two bedrooms and a small bathroom are being reconfigured to create the master suite. At Tom's insistence they will have an oversized shower where jets shoot water from all sides, massaging the muscles and easing the pain that comes with jogging and biking.

"I want the laundry room to be on the second floor where all the laundry is generated," Jennie commented.

"That's good planning, we can do that," Tom replied.

They decided their wisest investment would be updated wiring and plumbing. This increased the cost of the project substantially. Jennie defended the cost increase by saying, "Well, we aren't taking a vacation this year, so we'll put that money into the house."

Each day Tom tried to push away thoughts of all the work facing him before classes begin in a matter of days. He loves being involved in the renovation, and wants to be "on top of" everything going on so it was difficult to drag himself away.

He continued, "I've been thinking that the hand-carved limestone façade would look much better if we have it power washed to remove the years and years of city grime that has discolored the beautiful exterior. I'm going to get some bids on doing that work. If the cost is out of this world, we will put it off for a while."

"Yes, the limestone is dark and discolored – it would look more elegant if it had its original light color."

They were outside inspecting the facade and the condition of the limestone when an elderly gentleman who lives in the neighborhood and often walks by the house on his daily exercise routine stopped to chat. He told them he had been observing the renovation and wondered if they were happy with the results. It became obvious he was not satisfied to be engaged in idle conversation, but had something more important to say. Finally, as Jennie and Tom showed a lack of interest in his ramblings, he asked, "Do you know the history of your home?"

Naturally, Tom's curiosity was aroused, and he replied, "No, we only know that it was built in 1922."

The man seemed pleased that he could tell them something they didn't know and told them, "In 1930, a wealthy, older couple lived there, and it was rumored that they lost all their money in the crash. They lost everything including their will to live, and the man shot his wife and then shot himself. The house was vacant for a long number of years because it acquired a superstition and no one wanted to buy it. The house was too large for most people so it was made into a duplex sometime in the '40's when housing was in short supply. It's interesting that you are bringing it back to its original one-owner mansion. It was referred to as a mansion in its early days."

Tom and Jennie were speechless. They thanked the kind gentleman profusely and went inside to contemplate and digest his story. Then they burst out laughing at the thought of them unknowingly converting the duplex back to its original one-owner "mansion."

It was early in December when the last carpenter and the last painter picked up their tools and left, and gradually things returned to normal. Jennie and Tom were overjoyed with the results of the renovation that has been in progress since spring. There are some minor decorating projects yet to be done upstairs – Jennie says, "I think this house will always be a work in progress especially as Charlie grows."

Much of the success of the house is the result of diverse opinions. Suzanne had wonderful ideas; she could easily be a designer. At first, Jennie thought Tom would go along with everything she said, but no, he had strong opinions. For instance, since he was the "professional" cook in the house, he designed the kitchen so he could cook and still be able to converse with people when he is cooking. He wanted the kitchen to be a place for entertaining as well as cooking. He wanted it to be a place where people would gather and stay, not just a place to grab a bite and leave. The layout of the kitchen was a good two-hour long discussion over wine one evening. There wasn't a person who walked into this house who didn't admire the furnishings and the décor. To Jennie and Tom it is a source of comfort and pride.

It was completed just in time to show it off at their favorite Christmas party, the annual open house that has become a tradition. Everyone dresses, the ladies are festive and glittery, and the men suave and handsome. "We have lots of candles and delicious food. The sounds of popping corks and clinking spoons enliven the evening. We mingle and eat and talk – talks both serious and light-hearted – and then around midnight everyone leaves contented and entertained, and we all look forward to next year.

Even though Jennie had to cope with a renovation project that was constantly behind schedule and had to give into the demands of Charlie, she still found time to write. She just finished her fourth novel, **"The Man of her Dreams**." This was the first time her protagonist was a flawed character, and she constantly admonished her, but she went ahead and did things her way. The power of love is a strong one. It turned out to be a humorous exploit of the literary market, and Jennie said it was the most enjoyable novel she has written. She hoped Matt and Barnett would like it too.

As she entered Matt's office carrying her manuscript, his eyes lit up, and he rushed to greet her.

"I finally finished it, Matt, even though the dust settled on the pages as fast as I turned them."

"I'm a little surprised that you were able to even concentrate in that mess. But it was worth every bit of it, wasn't it? Suzanne almost moved in and took over seeing it through to completion. She loves that stuff."

Jennie laughed, "I was almost ready to hire her and give her the spare bedroom. She has great ideas. She helped me with the layout of my office. I love having my own office – if I need a break, I can polish my nails fire engine red or work Sudokus, or whatever. And, I can press those little yellow pads called Post-Its with wild abandon. To me they are a godsend and a recent innovation, but Tom says they have been around for years. Who cares, it's my office, and it can be as cluttered as I wish."

"Matt, I hope you like "**The Man of her Dreams**." I think it might be my best book. I had fun writing it so I have good feelings about it, and I hope Barnett feels the same way."

"If you feel that positive about it, I'm sure it will measure up. I can't wait to dig into it."

"I've gotten past the agony of rejections now, and I've learned something from each one of them. At first I felt the rejection was directed at me instead of my writing. I thought when I signed a publishing contract, my dream came true, and I could relax and bask in the glow of success."

"You're wrong – sure we instantly think of success, but then you become your own worst critic. We writers want each book to be better than the last, and that means hard work. And, as you know, a job or family put demands on our time, too. We are constantly under pressure as a deadline is always around the corner, so our butts need to be in a chair and our eyeballs staring at that piece of paper."

Jennie said, "I like the way you inject humor in the most serious situations."

"I didn't mean to be so blunt. Dreams are meant to be savored and enjoyed because of your hard work, but sometimes, the work can wait."

"Well, I'm anxious for your decision, so I'll leave. Thanks for all the advice that kept me focused and sane while I was reeling from Barnett's unfaltering barrage of criticisms."

Three weeks later, Jennie's confidence was again shattered. Matt told her that "Barnett didn't like the ending to **The Man of her Dreams**. He said that fiction novels always have a happy ending, and he didn't like the male protagonist, Brian Howard, going off to Tahiti and leaving Rachel in the lurch."

Matt further stated, "Jennie, Barnett is right; there is a written rule in the industry that women's fiction, which is your genre, and romance especially, have happy endings. Women are romantics, and for them love is the essence of life. They want their main characters to fall in love and live happily ever after. If the book doesn't have a happy ending they'll avoid buying that author's books in the future, so you have to rewrite the ending."

"You know, Matt, when I start a new book, I start off thinking this is going to be great; I'm so on top of it this time. Then when it's finished and it is sent to the publisher, I have a complete collapse of confidence – it's like taking two steps forward and four steps back. Did you ever go through that publishing seesaw?"

"No, I always had my father, who is a top-notch writer, read my work; he was very forthright, and I trusted his advice."

"Barnett said he did like the rest of the book and your sense of humor. He said you should inject more humor in your books."

When Jennie arrived home, Tom asked, "How'd it go?"

"Another rejection! I didn't expect that this time. But on the way home I thought about it, and I know how I will rewrite it: Rachel eventually realizes how shallow the egotistical Brian Howard is, and she yearns for her dream guy whose name is Mike. When Brian tells her he is going to Tahiti and wants her to go with him, she tells him she could never leave New York. (Inwardly, she wishes him bon voyage and good riddance.) One night she went to Bungalow 8, the Manhattan hangout where she met Mike, and, of course, he was there, but he was with another woman. They unknowingly begin to play a series of cat and mouse games. Mike decides to go to Bungalow 8 one night hoping to see Rachel. Of course, Rachel is there but she is with a date. On another occasion, she goes on a double date to a noisy pizzeria for a few beers. It's also another of her crowd's hang-outs. The first person she sees is Mike who is with a bunch of guys. A week or so later, she and her girl friends decided to drive to an upstate college town where a rock group from London was appearing. The lead singer was an emaciated drugged, glassy-eyed male whose hair that was braided in long dreadlocks flew about his head as he threw himself around the stage in reaction to the drums and deafening guitar chords amplified a thousand times.

The concert was a sell-out, and amid the clamor of thousands of shouting and writhing fans, she spotted Mike and ran to him. This time she would not let him get away. They eventually get back together and he instantly proposes. Of course, she accepts, and they live happily ever after.

Barnett liked the rewrite and the humorous capers Rachel and Mike put themselves through before finally realizing they are hopelessly in love and met for each other.

Chapter Twenty

Several years later Jennie was in her office mulling over the plot in her latest book when the phone rang. Writing was not going well, so the telephone, which would normally be an intrusion, was a welcome relief. The caller gave her name as Claire Ritchie from Harper Jones Publishing, and she stated: "For the 10th anniversary of '**A Brief Wondrous Life**', we would like to do a special re-release. It's done all the time. We give it a glossy new cover, a beautiful new author photo with an updated biography, and a whole new publicity campaign."

Jennie thought, "Well, they own the rights to it. It isn't as if I can stop them."

Claire continued, "We are hoping that you'd be available to help us promote it – maybe a six-city tour."

Jennie gulped and recovered, "There's no way I could go on a six-city tour with a child in elementary school. Could the tour be scheduled during the summer months? My husband is a college professor and his summers are free. I'll discuss it with him. Can I get back to you?"

"Yes, we can schedule it during the summer months. Just let me know what works best for you."

Tom was intrigued with the promotional tour, and he thought Jennie should agree to participate in the re-release of her first book. It would give her more exposure and help to keep her name before the public. The publicity will increase her future book sales.

"I think that's a wonderful offer; we'll all go on the tour – it will be a family vacation. While you are signing books, I'll keep Charlie occupied."

Jennie excitedly said, "That's what I was thinking," and she threw her arms around him. "I was afraid you would think it would be too costly for all of us to go. This is a professional dream come true. A writer can never get too much publicity."

When Jennie called Claire, she immediately sent a copy the book tour schedule to her. The tour will begin in Seattle, and then proceed to San Francisco, Los Angeles, Houston, New York City, and Chicago. She was impressed to learn that Claire Ritchie headed up the sales department at Harper Jones Publishing, and she would accompany Jennie on the tour. Matt will appear with Jennie at Borders in Chicago as he did for her initial book signing. It will be the final stop on the tour and a replay of the original signing of **A Brief Wondrous Life**. Agents also can never get too much publicity.

Jennie was not having a good night. She went to bed at ten and was now still awake at midnight counting the drops of rain that fell on top of the air conditioner that jutted out from the bedroom window. Tom was sleeping soundly beside her. Tomorrow they leave for Seattle, the first stop on her six-city book signing tour. They are packed and ready to leave at 7 o'clock in the morning, if only she could get some sleep. The excitement over the rerelease of **"A Brief Wondrous Life"** brought back memories of Steve, and the preparations left her exhausted.

Finally in a half-dream state, she gave in to her fatigue and slept soundly until Tom nudged her awake.

The flight to Seattle was non-stop and uneventful. Jennie entered the bookstore and was greeted by a display announcing the rerelease of **A Brief Wondrous Life.** Claire greeted her with a hug, and she seemed genuinely pleased to meet Jennie. It was evident to Jennie that Claire was from New York. She was strikingly tall and thin with thick short black hair. She wore a narrow long black skirt and an elegant white linen blouse that fit perfectly, and she was wearing 4" high heels. Shortly after arriving, she excused herself saying she would be back in a "jiff," and Jennie found her one failing. Claire smoked incessantly, and since smoking was not allowed in the bookstore, she constantly excused herself for another cigarette.

With her polished outward appearance, Jennie walked around the store smiling and mingling with customers. She looked slim and trim and glamorous in a black sleeveless dress with a trendy belt and a pair of black pumps with a sensible three-inch heel. It was an outfit she wore for many signings. She is an "old pro" at this now. She has always remembered the advice Matt gave her years ago: "When people have an opportunity to talk to an author, they will want to have a signed copy of their book." That has proved to be true! She always asks for the customer's name so she can personalize her autographed message to them. Claire was wonderful to work with and herself an "old pro." She graciously met the people as they entered the store, conversed with them, and introduced them to Jennie, "the best-selling author of **A Brief Wondrous Life**."

As they left the bookstore in Seattle, Jennie told her she was especially happy to be going to San Francisco, her favorite city. Claire confided to her that while in San Francisco she planned to have lunch with a friend from Tiburon, whom she called Bob, and since they were dear friends, their lunches sometimes continue into the evening.

When Jennie mentioned this to Tom, his eyes lit up, and he said, "Why don't we make the signing a family affair? Ten years ago when the book was first published, Jennie Rogers was single and a student at Columbia. I think your fans would like to see you today and meet your husband and son."

When they arrived in San Francisco, Tom gave Charlie a pep talk, telling him, "Today we are going to sell books for your mother. Afterward, we'll ride the trolley cars and go to the wharf."

The Grapevine bookstore in San Francisco was a great bookstore. Its clientele included aged hippies and starving artists who couldn't resist the inviting aroma of espresso. It had a wonderful smell, a mixture of newly printed books, a pleasant musky smell from the tons of used books, and the delicious smell of espresso. It was a place where one could browse for hours, and when Charlie left, he was carrying a large bag of used books.

When Claire left, Tom took over, and he was a handsome and attentive host. Jennie proudly stated, "I owe my continued success to my husband, Tom. He is my support and my mainstay. I wouldn't be where I am today if it were not for him." They celebrated a successful signing with dinner at Ernies.

The next morning Jennie was surprised to receive an early phone call and when she answered, in a sleepy, half-awake state, Claire was mumbling something about margarita's, Bob, late night, sorry luv, see you in Houston, and "click" she was gone. Jennie looked at Tom and laughingly related the sketchy conversation. "Will you help me sell books in L.A.?"

"Sure, we'll do a repeat performance in L.A. Claire is turning into an interesting person – think you'll ever hear the full story?"

"Probably not, but I think they were lovers at one time. He was transferred to the West Coast, and now they take advantage of every opportunity to be together. I think she knew all the time that they would be spending the night together at her hotel. I think it was all planned before she left New York; she would take advantage of the situation to be with her lover."

Sounds like you are describing the protagonist in one of your novels. Or, could she be in a future novel? But I think you are right, Claire wanted to escape with her lover for awhile."

Charlie piped in, "Are we going to sell books again in Los Angeles?"

"Yes, I'm afraid so, son, but we'll definitely go to the Space Center in Houston."

During lulls or quiet times in the store, Tom took Charlie on walks looking at store windows and ducking into stores of interest. They bought Knott's Berry Farm and Los Angeles Dodgers T-shirts at a sports store.

When Jennie arrived at the bookstore in Houston, Claire was there rearranging a display and talking with the manager. Jennie joined them, and for the rest of the day Claire did not say anything about her absence in San Francisco and Los Angeles, and neither did Jennie.

As Jennie later mentioned to Tom, "It's none of my business. In her job she doesn't have to answer to anyone. However, I liked seeing a human side to her."

"Yes, I did too – it was amusing to speculate about her private life."

Balloons outside the store in downtown Houston advertised the appearance of best-selling author, Jennie Rogers, and the rerelease of **A Brief Wondrous Life.** There was a steady stream of customers, particularly during the noon hour when office employees abandoned their offices to enliven their lunch hour.

The heat was an oppressive 98 degrees. "Maybe the air conditioning is luring them into the store," Jennie remarked.

"No, they are here to meet you and hopefully buy a book. Incidentally, how were the crowds in San Fran and LA?"

"We had good sales in San Fran, but sales in LA were weak. I hope we make up for it during the rest of the tour."

"I'm certain we will – the store in New York has been doing a bang-up job with publicity, so I expect sales to be brisk. They always do a good job for Harper Jones."

"Matt has some great promotions going on in Chicago. He will try his best to do a good job there with Borders Books & Music. That is where he launched my book ten years ago."

"Yes, I recall that, Jennie, we knew you would become a best seller. Incidentally, I've been wondering if this rerelease of your book about Steve has been difficult for you, like opening an old wound."

"No, in the past ten years a lot has happened. The FBI indicated that when Steve went undercover to get enough evidence to convict Nathan Roth, he was successful, but before he had the opportunity to testify against him, Roth had him killed. The FBI and the media were unrelenting in their search for everyone involved in Steve's murder. I was very bitter for a long time but now that the killers are behind bars, I feel vindicated. There have been times when I thought I would like to write a sequel telling the whole story and the truth, but others have done a tremendous amount of research and have written a fair analysis of the case so I'll just let it be."

At 5 o'clock, Claire said she was calling it a day, and she asked Jennie what her plans were.

Jennie said, "I'll stay here until Tom and Charlie get here. They are touring the Space Center today."

"You may have a long wait," Claire cautioned.

"That's okay. I have a few books to sign. I want Charlie to see as much as he can today."

"Okay, I'll see you in New York."

Thirty minutes later, Tom and Charlie entered the store. "Mom, you should have seen the space shuttle – it is huge," Charlie eagerly informed her, "It's as tall as a building!"

"We'll go back some day when we can all go, there's much more to see and do," Tom said.

"Well, my day was profitable so I had fun, too. We had good traffic and sold lots of books. It will be interesting to see what happens in New York."

They had just entered the Barnes and Noble bookstore in Manhattan when a black Lincoln Town Car pulled up, and Claire stepped out and walked into the store. As Jennie learned later, it was one of a fleet of Town Cars owned by Harper Jones, and one would be at their disposal to drive them wherever they wished to go.

Claire looked gorgeous in a black silk skirt that skimmed her knees and a lemon-lime silk blouse and black sandals. She tossed a hand-beaded tote bag on the counter as though it was an insignificant canvas tote when in reality it probably could have paid her rent for a year.

"Claire, thank you for the use of the car — Tom will certainly appreciate that as we are strangers to New York."

"At Harper Jones, we treat our customer's right!"

And, Claire was right. They certainly did a "bang-up" publicity campaign. A make-up artist appeared and then a reporter and a photographer from CITY magazine arrived to interview Jennie. Everywhere were banks of fresh-cut flowers and pyramids of Jennie's book. Jennie was amazed at the steady influx of patrons who came to meet "a favorite author", and she was happy to meet and converse with everyone. She was overjoyed with the reception she received in New York, and she knew its success was due to Claire.

Later in the day, Claire announced she had to leave early because of an appointment. She hugged Jennie and thanked her for participating in the book tour. She said she wouldn't be going to Chicago as Matt would take charge of the final stop on the tour.

Jennie again thanked her for everything, and she hoped the tour would pay off with increased future sales of the book. Claire was confident the book would continue to sell well.

Soon the Town Car pulled up in front of the store, and Tom stepped out to pick up Jennie. "That's the only way to see New York," he remarked. He had gotten to know the driver quite well, and he introduced Jennie to him saying, "James will drop us off at our hotel, and then we will be on our own. He recommended a small restaurant two blocks from the hotel where we can discuss the day's activities over dinner."

Jennie was happy to be back home and back to familiar surroundings. When she entered Borders bookstore in Chicago, her mind went back to the book's publication and her first signing. It took place at this same store, and she glanced at the same colorful poster in the window advertising **A Brief Wondrous Life**, the book she wrote as a way of coping with the sorrow of Steve's death. On that day she wondered if anyone would be interested enough to buy her book. Now, ten years later, the book which became a best seller, is being re-released, and she wonders if a new generation of readers will be interested enough to buy her book. Sales at the other bookstores on the tour went well so she is optimistic. She smiled and cheerfully greeted the rush of customers as the doors opened for business. Matt's knowing smile gave her the assurance she needed.

The line of people waiting, hoping to have a word with her as she signed their books was steady, and she became consumed with the task at hand. The day continued in that manner, and Matt's consummate skill as a host and agent reinforced the day's huge success.

Matt asked Jennie about a fifth book, and she told him she has been working on it since Tom was hospitalized. She hasn't finalized all the details yet as she's trying to connect it with Tom's ordeal. It's about a man who suffered a head injury in an accident, and he was in a coma for six and one half months. His doctors held no hope of him recovering, and if he did he would have brain damage and be in a nursing home until his death. In the meantime, his wife met someone, they fell in love, and considered marriage, but for religious reasons, the wife held back. Later her husband came out of the coma, but, as the doctors suspected, he suffered severe brain damage. No one could predict how long he would live. The name of the book is **"Together Again."**

Matt asked, "How will it end?"

Jennie replied, "I'm wrestling with that now."

"Be careful – you have to consider the adultery issue – heroes and heroines don't commit adultery. You don't want to have a bunch of moralists boycotting your book."

"Yes, Matt, I've thought about that. I read a story about a similar case where the husband unexpectedly came out of a coma and lived or existed for some time, and then he went into late stage Alzheimers and eventually died in his sleep. His wife had met someone else and fell in love, but she put her life on hold and continued to visit him in the nursing home until his death even though the doctors had told her he would never regain consciousness."

"My main reason for writing the book was to bring to light a medical condition that does happen but is usually swept under the rug. It's a real life situation that deserves to be told. I almost had to deal with it personally when Tom was in a coma."

"I can certainly relate to your interest in writing about that subject. We all were on pins and needles the whole time Tom was in the hospital. Sounds like you've done your research, and it will be an interesting book."

One Saturday Tom came inside leafing through the mail that had just been delivered, and he pulled out an envelope and handed it to Jennie saying, "This one's for you."

Jennie hurriedly scanned the return address and remarked, "I'm not interested in that" and tossed it aside. The return address read, "Quincy All-School Reunion."

"But Jennie it's your high school reunion in Quincy – how can you say that?"

"I'm just not interested in another reunion." The mention of a high school reunion brings back memories of Steve and the image of his body lying in a pool of blood. The word reunion brings back a flood of unpleasant memories, and she still wondered if Steve would be alive today if she hadn't gone to her tenth year reunion without him. She remembers how hurt he was when she told him she wanted to go alone. Now they were proposing a twenty-year reunion.

"Why not, Jennie?"

She thought to herself, "He doesn't know what I go through when I think of that reunion, and I can't explain it to him."

"Jennie, you have made a name for yourself in Quincy, and everyone will expect to see you. If you don't show up people will think because you have written four books, you are too big a star to attend your high school reunion. I think you should go and show them that you are a local Quincy girl who made good and is proud of it. Let's go and have a good time. I know Lynn and Roger will expect us to be there."

Jennie knew it was the proper thing to do, and she nonchalantly said, "Well, since you put it that way, let's go."

They drove the familiar four hour drive to Quincy and arrived in time for the annual football game with Macomb, Quincy's rival, and they barely eked out a victory. Then they found their way to the old Holiday Inn that has become home to Quincy's reunion dinner dances. Most everyone knew of Jennie's success, and they were eager to greet her and congratulate her on her success as, "Quincy's famous author.

As she scanned the crowd looking for familiar faces, half the faces looked as if they were the "later" version of "then and later" faces drawn by a police artist. The rest were instantly recognizable, and she smiled and waved a greeting.

While dancing with Tom, she commented, "It's interesting to watch people's eyes as they scrutinize you like they're not sure what they should say, so they merely say, "Hey, you look great."

Jennie continued, "I remember the tenth reunion everyone was comparing themselves to each other trying to see who was more successful. Now they are bragging about their children and their plans for retirement."

"Yes, everyone has mellowed, they are complacent with their niche in life and are no longer competing for status and wealth. They have nothing to prove. They came just because they wanted to see old friends again. And, as you readily noticed, we have all aged."

"Yes," Jennie replied as she looked around the room. "In spite of the gray heads and pot bellies, everyone looks happy. Our twentieth reunion is much different than our tenth. Youthful pretensions have been replaced by the maturity that comes with marriage and kids. We have a different rapport with each other – it's all about our future and what's left of it, not our adolescent years that can never be relived because we aren't the same persons we were in high school that we are now. We are all living in the present, and we are happy with our lives today, not realizing we are growing older."

While Roger and Tom were in a deep conversation with some other guys, Jennie and Lynn went off for a moment by themselves. Jennie confided to her "I didn't want to come to the reunion, but Tom pressured me into coming. I thought the memories of Steve and the last reunion would be too painful to endure, but I've gotten past that and I'm glad we came."

"Well, I'm certainly glad you came. Incidentally, did you ever find out what happened or why Steve was murdered?"

"Yes, I stayed in touch with Steve's parents, and naturally they were aware of all the investigative work, so they were up-to-date on everything. They had close to a hundred newspaper clippings in which Steve's name was mentioned. We learned that Steve was asked by the FBI to change his identity, go undercover, and accept a job with Nathan Roth, in order to infiltrate the mob and learn their connections to the state construction projects in Arizona.

"Steve agreed to this dangerous assignment, and he accepted the job of chief accountant to Nathan Roth. Roth put him up in a rent-free, designer-decorated condominium, and he was given the keys to a company car. Of course, microphones and transmitters had been planted in the walls of every room in the condo. The car was also wired, so they had a tail on him day and night, and, of course, they knew who he talked to and what was said."

"Two days before the court date, Steve was sitting in a bar with an FBI agent, sharing his apprehensions, saying, "What am I going to do, what am I going to say when I get called to testify?' To diminish his fears, he tried to downplay his role, "I have done nothing wrong. I can't tell them anything they don't already know." But, in reality, he was in serious trouble, and he knew it. Of course, he didn't know that the young woman who was seated next to him at the bar and making a play for the bartender, had been hired to spy on him so Roth was aware of Steve's assignment. As a result, he was gunned down the following day before he had a chance to testify."

Ongoing investigations revealed that Steve had received a letter in the mail a day before the scheduled hearings before the grand jury which read, "You're Next." That was all it said. Evidently Steve shrugged it off as a prank; after all he did have witness protection. However, he had secretly testified before another grand jury a few days earlier and that evidently prompted the threat.

"The FBI didn't think they killed him for what he might say in further testimony. Steve was a minor character in the scheme of things, and they think he was killed to deter others from testifying. Steve was expendable; they think he was killed simply to show others they could do it and would."

"The FBI was berated for not giving Steve protection the day before the trial. It was later determined that they did offer Steve protection, but Steve didn't think it was necessary; he couldn't believe a person would go around shooting someone for no reason. This wasn't the Wild West as Arizona was sometimes referred to in jest – this was 1972! The press further admonished the FBI saying they should have insisted that Steve be put in a 'safe house' or even an overnight stay in jail for protection."

"The County District Attorney was particularly bitter about Steve's murder as Steve was the state's star witness, and his testimony would have been enough to bring charges against Roth. However, the FBI refused to give up, and a month later new charges were filed against Roth and this time they were able to convict him. One of Roth's associates told the FBI that he had the ability to pick up the phone and have a person killed. Roth was given life, but a few months after his conviction, he suffered a serious heart attack and was given 3 to 5 years to live. After three years, he died in prison cell #31509, so Steve's murder was finally avenged. The two thugs hired to kill him were Chicago mafia hit men, and they were eventually caught and jailed on other charges as well as Steve's murder. They were given life, but one was murdered in the jail's kitchen by another inmate. They say he was afraid for his life all during his incarceration. The other guy is still in prison as far as I know."

"We were told that the dime placed on Steve's forehead was a trademark of the Chicago mafia. We also learned that the two hit men were paid $10,000 for taking Steve's life – can you imagine putting a price of $10,000 on a person's life. They didn't even know who Steve was or why they were killing him; they killed him because they were ordered to do so. It didn't matter that Steve was only 28 years old, a nice, normal guy who was just trying to do his job. It was difficult for Steve's family and friends to make sense of it all – for his death to seem real – hit men in a stairwell – broad daylight – someone ordering them to kill – it was like a B movie!"

"Steve's parents had to suffer through all of the investigations. It was very difficult for them to cope with all that his murder involved. They were grief-stricken for a long time. Steve was very close to his parents."

Lynn said, "That was an awful thing to happen to anybody, and I've always wondered if Steve didn't suspect that something like that could happen to him since he was up against the mafia."

"Yes, I'm sure he thought about it. When he said, 'Always know that I love you,' I think he was very aware of the dangerous situation he was in, but he bravely continued to do what he had to do to help the FBI in their investigations. What he didn't know was that no one worked for Nathan Roth and left his company alive."

"For a long time I had feelings of guilt over the class reunion thing. Even though I know we can't live in hindsight or look back and blame ourselves for things that can't be corrected, I took the blame and grieved. But I discovered that the closure survivors need isn't catching the criminals, it's the time that is needed for healing the heartache so they can move on with life, and I learned that the feeling of guilt is a normal step in the grieving process. I can live with Steve's murder now. It's like a dark cloud blew away, and now I only see light."

When they were home and settled in bed, Tom asked, "Now aren't you glad you went?" She replied, "Yes, Darling, it makes me appreciate you so much more."

Sometime later, Tom and Jennie were having dinner with Matt and Suzanne, and Matt said that Bob Barnett at Harper Jones told him they had just bought the first novel of an up-and-coming young writer whose novel was great, and she would become a best seller "every bit as good as Jennie Rogers."

"Well, that certainly calls for a toast," Tom said as he signaled for the waiter.

The following day, Jennie was downtown shopping, and she ducked into Borders bookstore. As she was looking through the new releases for the book which Matt mentioned while having dinner, she overheard the conversation of a nearby shopper to her friend, "That's Jennie Rogers, the author. She wrote **A Brief Wondrous Life**. You should read it."